MOG AND T

Mog is the greatest leader a gang ever had; Mog's hero is the Rectifier. Mog's plans to follow in the footsteps of this mysterious Robin Hood figure are continually thwarted by spoilt rich-kid Howard Bygrave and his sinister chauffeur Mr Skin. By chance they all get involved with the Rectifier's plans, and something that starts as a game suddenly becomes serious.

A tangle of crises develops and somehow the powerful, elusive figure of the Rectifier is behind it all ...

About the author

Chris Powling was born and brought up
in South London, where he now lives
with his wife and two daughters. He has
taught at all levels, from infants to
under-graduates and is currently a
headteacher at a London primary
school. He has been a reviewer of
children's books for some time, and
has been a contributor to the radio
programme *Kaleidoscope*, which he also
presents during the holidays. He is the
author of several children's books,
published in both paperback and
hardback.

Mog and the Rectifier

Chris Powling

Illustrated by Stephen Lavis

KNIGHT BOOKS
Hodder and Stoughton

For Jan

Copyright © Chris Powling 1980
Illustrations © Hodder & Stoughton Ltd 1982
First published by Abelard-Schuman Ltd 1980
First published by Knight Books 1982

British Library C.I.P.

Powling, Chris
  Mog and the Rectifier.
  I. Title
  823'.914[J]   PZ7

  ISBN 0-340-28046-8

Printed and bound in Great Britain for
Hodder and Stoughton Paperbacks, a
division of Hodder and Stoughton Ltd.,
Mill Road, Dunton Green, Sevenoaks,
Kent (Editorial Office: 47 Bedford
Square, London, WC1 3DP) by
Cox & Wyman Ltd, Reading

Dear Reader

Everything described in these pages happened about two years ago. It's important for me to tell you this because I still blame myself for what I did. How much will you blame me, I wonder?

Also, I wonder how you'll feel about The Rectifier? To some people, like my Dad, he's a hero. To others he's not much better than a nutcase. What are we supposed to think of someone who steals paintings and jewellery and money — but only from rich cheats who should have handed them over to the Government in the first place? After all, everything he takes gets sent straight to the Inland Revenue, which is the government department that gathers our taxes so we can pay for hospitals and schools and roads and the army and so on. When each parcel arrives with the usual note — 'Collected For The Government by The Rectifier' — the tax-inspectors never know whether to laugh or cry.

But who is The Rectifier? How does he operate?

This is a story about him.......or nearly about him. In fact it's about a group of kids who saw him in action. I was one of them — that's right me, a scrawny, shy bookworm with only two real interests in life. One was to win a Scholarship to a posh, public school so that one day I'd become a professor or a brain-surgeon or prime-minister. The other was to please our gang-leader, Mog Catley.

Mog was special.

Yes, Mog was just as special as my Scholarship. That's why the worst moment of my life was when I had to choose between the two. And that's why, in this account, I, call myself 'Genius' or 'Brains' or 'Scholarship Boy' which is what Mog and Lenny and Alex and all the other kids called me. Nowhere do I tell you my true name because even now, a couple of years later, I'm too ashamed.

Yours faithfully,
Genius.

On the Bridge

From the railway bridge down to the railway line you'd fall about fifteen feet. This was enough to kill you, Mog said. Even if it wasn't then the electric rail would frizzle you to death or you'd be crushed by a passing train. So you had to be a daredevil or daft to climb over one of the parapets of the bridge, cling by toetip and fingertip to the outside ledges and work your way to the middle. Yet here was Mog doing it—and all to rescue a small, scruffy bird.

One mistake and Mog would be dead. The rest of us watched from the embankment. We were so quiet we could hear the wind in the telegraph wires and the rustle of the nettles and dock-leaves that covered the slope. When Mog's foot slipped and scattered bits of brick on the track it sounded like a warning that Mog would be next. Still Mog kept going.

"It's a mad thing to try," Lenny declared. "A sparrow's not worth it."

"Mog doesn't think so," I said.

Lenny shook his head glumly.

"It's too risky even for Mog."

As if to prove him right Mog had stopped. Soon we knew why. A train was coming.

"It's the 6.17 from Cannon Street," said Alex. "My dad might be on it."

"And Mog might be under it," muttered Lenny.

We were almost too scared to breathe in case we loosened Mog's grip. The clatter and thud of the train got louder as it rounded the bend.

"Will it shake the bridge?" Alex said.

"Quiet!" Lenny hissed.

Mog was flat against the brickwork spread like a bat or a four-legged spider. We saw the train a split second before it reached the bridge, then its first carriage was under and out and alongside and past us with carriage after carriage to follow, each a couple of feet below Mog's feet.

". . . six, seven, eight, nine . . ." I counted.

Nine was the last carriage and the rush of the train faded. Mog was still on the bridge.

"Give up now," pleaded Alex.

"No point," Lenny said. "Not when you're almost there. Might as well finish the job."

Not that Mog would have given up anyway as we well knew.

"Okay, Mog," I said. "Take it carefully . . . bend slowly to the ledge . . . scoop up the bird . . . steady . . . you've done it! Now have a breather . . ."

"Hark at the expert," scoffed Lenny. "Done a lot of this sort of thing have you?"

I tried to smile.

"Never have, never will. Not without a safety-net."

"Safety-net? What . . . for the train to bash into? Fat lot of good a safety-net would be. You've got to do it Mog's way or not at all."

This was true of most things Mog did.

"Good old Mog," Alex chuckled. "Takes more than a train to beat Mog."

"What about a catapult?" said Lenny suddenly.

"Eh?"

"A catapult. Fired by Howard Bygrave. He's over there."

Lenny pointed to the opposite slope. There was Howard Bygrave. Also Mr Skin, Howard's chauffeur. As always Mr Skin wore black—black boots, black uniform, black gloves and helmet, black vizor. For once we weren't looking at him, though. Howard's catapult had all our attention. Its elastic stretched from his fist to his shoulder as he took careful aim at Mog.

"He's bluffing," said Alex. "He wouldn't dare."

"He would," said Lenny. "He hates Mog enough."

"Mog will fall, though. It'll be murder. We'll be witnesses."

"Who'd believe us?" I asked. "It would be our word against Howard's—and he'll have a grown-up on his side."

"He wouldn't dare," Alex insisted.

But Howard would dare anything while he had Mr Skin to back him up. The catapult twanged. Too fast for us to see it the stone smacked into the parapet six inches from Mog's head.

"Stop that!" shrieked Alex.

Howard bent casually for another stone. He held it up for us to see. With no stones on our side of the cutting and with the railway between us he knew there was nothing we could do. We heard his high-pitched voice singing.

"Humpty-Moggy sat on the wall. Humpty-Moggy had a great fall . . ."

Sneering, he turned back to his target. What he saw astonished him—and us. One handed, feet shuffling, Mog was moving to the end of the bridge fast. Not to our end of the bridge though: Mog was after Howard.

Howard was so surprised he misfired. The stone hit his own fist. He screeched with pain and dropped the catapult. By then Mog was on the embankment.

"Skin! Skin!" Howard yelped. "Do something!"

Mr Skin sprang forward but Mog was too quick and too angry to be caught. The chauffeur found himself clutching at nothing as Mog side-stepped and stuck out a foot. Hardly believing it, we saw Mr Skin sprawl headlong. By the time he'd got back on his feet, Mog had the stone and the catapult and Howard. Mog didn't speak loudly but we could hear every word.

"Get rid of him . . . or this stone will be down your throat and your teeth with it."

"Don't fire it!" Howard begged. "Please don't fire it."

"Get rid of him."

"All right—all right! Go away, Skin. Wait . . . er . . . wait for me by the bike." Mr Skin straightened his helmet but stayed where he was. Mog just straightened the catapult. Howard's voice became a babble.

"Go away, you fool! Go away! Go away!"

Without a word the chauffeur saluted, swivelled and climbed the slope. Not until he'd gone did Mog speak.

"Now dig."

"What?"

"Dig. Dig a hole."

"What with?"

"With your hands."

Howard stared at his chubby, pink hands and perfect finger-nails.

"How . . . how big does it have to be?" he asked.

"I'll tell you when to stop," Mog said. "Now dig."

His face green, Howard began to scrape at the dirt. Each time he looked up and stared into the long V of elastic with the stone at the end of it he whimpered and dug more frantically.

"What's Mog doing?" asked Lenny. "Making him dig his own grave?"

"It's for the bird," I said.

When the mound of earth was sandcastle-size with a hole to match, Mog lowered the catapult.

"Get going," said Mog.

Howard edged away then turned and ran, blubbering with relief. The instant he was out of sight we heard the sound we all hated—like a robot having a tantrum, Mog called it. Mr Skin and started a thousand ccs of motor bike.

"Good riddance," said Lenny.

Mog knelt down. From where we were it looked like a handful of fluff being covered up.

"Takes more than a train to beat you, Mog," Alex declared later. "Takes more than a catapult and Howard and Mr Skin, too. Wait till we tell them at school what happened!"

"Make sure you tell them right then," Mog said. "Including the stupid bit."

"What stupid bit?"

"The bird. It was already dead when I picked it up."

"That wasn't the stupid bit," Lenny snorted. "The stupid bit was trying a climb like that in the first place whether the bird was alive or dead. It was . . . it was . . ."

"Disproportionate," I suggested.

"Okay, Brains," said Lenny. "If that means it wasn't worth what might've happened."

"I didn't think what might've happened *would* happen," Mog explained. "And it didn't."

Lenny sighed.

"The trouble with you, Mog, is that you think you've got nine lives."

"Would you really have fired that stone down Howard's throat?" asked Alex.

"How could I? The catapult was broken when I picked it up. From Howard mucking up his shot, I suppose. What are you looking at me like that for?"

We were looking at Mog like that because we couldn't believe it.

"You mean . . . you mean you were threatening Howard with a catapult that wouldn't fire?" said Lenny faintly.

"Yes. But Howard and Mr Skin didn't know that. I was holding it so they couldn't see."

I let out a whoop of delight.

"Wait till we tell them *that* at school! That's the not-so-stupid bit. That's the brilliant bit!"

"That's the brilliant bit!" echoed Alex.

We laughed all the way up the hill. Especially me because I still couldn't believe my luck in being a member of the gang at all. At the top we turned as we always did and looked back over the steeples and cranes and tower-blocks and houses and greenery. Down on the river a boat sounded its horn as if it were joining in the joke. Howard may have had a rich dad and a huge motorbike with a chauffeur to drive it, but we had Mog. Mog was the best leader a gang ever had. Even if she was a girl.

Two Entrances

Even if she was a girl, Mog took the lead in everything we did. She didn't *try* to be Big Chief, it just happened. Here's an example—the Monday we first met Mr. Skin and Howard's glittering machine.

Howard arrived at school like a knight in leather armour. His boots and breeches were leather and so were his jacket and gauntlets. At first we didn't recognise him at all beneath the dome-shaped crash-helmet. This was also trimmed with leather. Only when the motor bike pulled into the kerb and he lifted the see-through vizor did we know who it was. The growl of the engine died away.

"It's Howard!" exclaimed Alex.

Lenny gave a long whistle.

"Look at that machine! It's as big as a horse."

"It's about as long as a horse," I said. "But it's only half as high."

"All right, Genius," Lenny replied. "It's also about ten times more powerful."

"Ten times more powerful than a horse?" said Alex. "Give over!"

"Lenny's right," I said. "It's a thousand cc—ten horse-power."

This time it was Alex who whistled. By now Howard had an audience of about two hundred kids. Most of the mums in the Infant playground next door were watching too. Howard loved it. He stayed right where he was while Mr Skin dismounted and lifted the bike on to its stand. With Howard's weight as well this couldn't have been easy but Mr Skin made it look as if he were parking a scooter.

"Who's he?" Alex asked.

"The new Bygrave chauffeur, I suppose," sniffed Lenny. "Don't like the look of him much."

"There's not much of *him* you could like the look of," I pointed out. "All you can see is helmet and uniform."

"About seven feet of helmet and uniform," said Lenny. "That's what I don't like: Howard's private giant."

We shuddered at the thought. Especially as Howard was making it clear who was in charge. He took off his gloves slowly and handed them to Mr Skin. Unbuckling his helmet took even longer.

"Fetch my shoes, Skin," he ordered.

These were in one of the bike's dispatch-cases. Mr Skin unzipped Howard's boots and his leather breeches. Beneath them Howard's trousers were scarcely creased except where they should be creased. Mr Skin helped Howard on with his shoes and a cream windcheater that was lined with cream fur. No kid we knew was better dressed than Howard. Or snootier. All the time he tilted his nose as if one sniff of Mr Skin or anyone else would be enough to poison him.

"Pack the gear carefully, Skin. Remember it cost money."

"Yes, sir."

The chauffeur's voice had a sub-zero coldness.

"I expect I'll have to do some writing about the bike in class today, Skin. So just remind me of a few facts, will you?"

"Certainly, sir."

"What's its designation?"

"GL 1000-K2, sir. It's a water-cooled, flat-four, four-stroke with an overhead camshaft."

"And the clutch?"

"Semi-wet multi-plate, sir."

"With five-speed constant-mesh transmission?"

"That's correct, sir."

"What about the brakes?"

"Hydraulically operated, sir. Twin disc on the front, single disc on the rear."

"Probably I'll need some figures, too, Skin," Howard drawled. "Tell me about the bore and the stroke."

Lenny gave a snort of disgust.

"Howard's the bore," he declared.

"And the stroke's what I'd like to give him," said Alex. "Across his fat backside."

"He's still got everyone looking and listening though," I said. "Even the little kids who don't understand a word of it."

"Never mind the little kids," said Lenny, "*I* don't understand a word of it. Do you?"

"Only some," I admitted.

On and on went Howard in his posh, piping voice as he tried to dazzle us with science and riddle us with jealousy. He brought up gear ratios and compression ratios, maximum power and torque power, plus the bike's capacity, kerb weight, length, width and height. We even found out that its frame was tubular steel and double-cradle whatever that meant.

"You know I'm beginning to get the idea that there's a teeny-weeny bit of the show-off about Howard," Lenny remarked. "Of course, I could be wrong."

"You must be wrong," said Alex. "Because Howard's *perfect*. A kid told me."

"Which kid was that?"

"Howard."

"Silly me," said Lenny. "Fancy forgetting that Howard's perfect."

All this was said loud enough for Howard to hear though there wasn't much chance he'd be listening. He was too busy trying to amaze us.

"And how much *was* the bike, Mr Skin?" he asked.

"Nineteen hundred and ninety-five pounds, sir," the chauffeur replied. "With more for the extras, of course."

"Of course," said Howard.

"Of course," Lenny mimicked. "I mean, you wouldn't expect a mere two thousand blinking quid for a motor bike to *include* the extras, would you? That would be doing it on the cheap. He's probably bought two . . . an extra model for when this one gets dirty."

"I wouldn't mind one," I admitted.

Lenny looked at me savagely.

"You could always make friends with Howard."

I shrugged and grinned to show that this was too high a price to pay. But was it? I began to wonder . . . along with a couple of hundred other kids who were eyeing Howard's latest toy.

Then Mog came.

She arrived so suddenly and so strangely that in an instant she had every boy and every girl looking her way. Even the mums and Howard and Mr Skin stood staring. Mog came down the slope on the far side of the brick wall that curved round the playground. All we could see were her feet. Yet they were Mog's feet for sure. We knew that even before we recognised her falling-to-bits plimsolls.

Mog's feet jogged along above the height of the wall as if she were in mid-air only upside-down. The brickwork hid her—except for her shins and shoes.

"I don't get it," Lenny muttered. "She must be . . ."

". . . walking on her hands," breathed Alex.

"She can't be," I said. "That's circus stuff."

It was circus stuff. Where the wall became a chain-link fence Mog came into view. Her back was bent, her legs were spread for balance and she put one hand in front of the other with as much sureness and speed as if they were boots and she were the right way up. With her body curved and her head tipped up to see where she was going she looked like a scorpion about to strike. This was odd because there was nothing deadly about Mog. Compared with most kids Mog was a softy.

Especially compared with Howard. Right now his face ought to have shrivelled up from the look he had on it. Once again he'd been outdone by Mog.

Her hands slap-slapped along the pavement and through the school gates. Once she was in the playground she paused, bunched a bit, then flipped over so she was standing upright. Alex clapped first. Soon we were all clapping, even some of the mums. Mog bowed and curtsied and blew kisses but somehow you could tell she wasn't really bothered what people thought about her gymnastics. She was just pleased to be able to do them at all. By the time the school bell rang the hand-walking season was established. Boys and girls of all sizes and shapes were head-standing and handstanding and somersaulting and forward-and-backward rolling as they tried to copy Mog. Not a single kid was pretending to ride a motorbike.

"I just can't get the hang of it," Alex complained. "How come you can do it, Mog?"

"Practice," said Mog. "Weeks of it. My mum showed me."

Alex nodded briskly and looked away. We all looked away. We always did when Mog spoke about her mum.

"Hey," Mog said. "There's Howard over there!"

"Didn't you see him?" Lenny asked. "As you went past him he practically took a bite out of your leg."

"Didn't notice him at all. I was concentrating on getting here."

"He came on that motor bike," I said. "With a chauffeur to match."

"Called Mr Skin," said Alex.

"How come you know his name?" Mog asked.

"Howard introduced him," Lenny said. "To us and all the other kids in the playground. He also gave us a run-down on just about every nut and bolt on the bike.

You arrived in the middle of it. And that didn't make Howard happy."

"Poor old Howard," laughed Mog. "He can't stand being upstaged."

"Being what?"

"Upstaged. It's a mean thing some actors do. They sort of hog the audience's attention. My mum's told me about it."

Again the mention of Mog's mum was enough to make Lenny's face and Alex's face and my face go blank.

"You didn't do it on purpose, though," said Alex quickly.

"Howard will think I did."

"Who cares what Howard thinks?"

"I do," said Mog.

And she meant it. She really meant it. From anyone else it would have sounded sarcastic but not from Mog.

This was the side of our gang leader that was hardest for kids to understand. After a while you got over the shock of her being a girl. Yet how come she was so nice? She didn't spit, she didn't swear, she didn't hit first—she didn't even hit back if she could avoid it. Howard once called her 'sweet'. She was too sweet to pick her own nose, he sneered. Mog grinned and nodded and said she was happy to leave her share of nose-picking to Howard providing he kept to his own nose. This was quite a clever answer, we thought. But we'd have preferred her to bash Howard up which she could have done easily. After all, what kind of a gang leader is a goody-goody?

Mog's kind . . . and our kind, apparently. Luckily most kids liked and admired her so much her niceness didn't bother them. When you're goalkeeper for the school football team, shooter for the netball team, play rounders and cricket for the school and can outrun, outjump, outbalance and outswim everyone else in the school, then you can get away with being nice.

And as if all this wasn't enough, Mog was good at

lessons, too. Only one person was quicker at maths, more clever with words and could draw better than Mog and that person was me. Inside the classroom I was first, Mog was second and Howard Bygrave was third. Outside the classroom Mog was first every time—with Howard and me out of sight. He was too fat and I was too weedy. Mog alone was superb at work *and* play. Mog was Superkid.

Yes, Katharine Catley was Superkid. We all admitted that. Where did she get it from? Certainly not from her mum.

Mrs Catley

Mog's mum spent her time staring out of the window. Not some of her time or even most of her time. So far as we knew—Lenny and Alex and me, that is—she spent *all* her time staring out of the window.

"Who do you reckon does the housework, then?" asked Alex.

"Simple," said Lenny, "Mog does."

"What, everything? All the cooking and cleaning and washing?"

"And the shopping," I added.

"We all have to do shopping," said Alex, ruefully.

"Not the whole lot and the rest of the housework too," Lenny said. "Mog's mum doesn't lift a finger—except to beckon Mog when she wants something."

"And she's got no visible means of support," I said.

"Eh?" said Alex. "Sounds rude."

"Okay, Scholarship Boy," Lenny sighed. "What does that mean?"

I shrugged. "It's just a phrase. To do with the law, I think. It means no one knows where her money comes from. What she lives on. She doesn't draw Social Security because Mog would have to collect it for her. Yet she doesn't seem to work."

"Work?" snorted Lenny. "She doesn't even get up! She just lies there in that sort of dragon-thing like a beautiful princess who's fading away."

Lenny was right. That was just the way Mog's mum looked. It was the only way we'd ever seen her—in the same dressing gown of chinese silk, on the same sofa, in the same room overlooking the garden. The window curved round her from floor to ceiling so she had a good view. Once, before the house was turned into flats, it must have been worth seeing. Today there was the railway embankment and the backs of a terrace of houses and our school with its scatter of classrooms all on different levels. Only the trees were left. So what did Mog's mum find to stare at?

"Perhaps she's thinking," I suggested.

"Thinking?" said Alex. "What about?"

"Well, perhaps she's a writer or a painter or some kind of mad genius who can do all her work at home."

"Wouldn't Mog have told us if her mum was any of those?" asked Lenny. "Strikes me there's something strange about Mrs Catley. Haven't you heard the stories—that she's been seen slinking back into the house late at night or in the early morning? And if you believed all the things she's supposed to have taught Mog she must be a cross between Houdini and Batman."

"Mog's never actually said anything like that," I pointed out.

"She sort of hints it though. Does Mog make her sound like a normal mum? Does she do anything a normal mum does? Except have a lie-in on a Sunday morning, that is."

Alex laughed.

"With Mrs Catley every morning is Sunday morning!"

"Too true," agreed Lenny.

"The worst of it is we can't even ask her," I said. "How do you ask someone if their mum is as bone-idle as she seems? Especially when Mog always treats her as some kind of a heroine. You know Mog!"

"Do we?" Lenny said. "Do we really know Mog? She makes you feel she's been around all your life organising everything and daredevilling all over the place. But she didn't turn up at school till just before the end of the

Summer term. That's only about ten months ago."

"Is that all?" said Alex. "It feels like forever."

"Exactly," said Lenny.

"What does it matter?" I asked. She's here now and she's gang leader good and proper. Or do you think it's you who should be gang leader?"

For a moment I thought I'd gone too far. Beneath his carrotty fringe Lenny's flat, pug-like face scowled. Then he grinned.

"Never. Not with Mog around. I can't compete with Mog. But Genius, me old mate . . ."

"Yes?"

He lifted a finger and tapped me softly on the nose.

"Just watch that lip of yours. All right?"

I swallowed.

"All right."

"Here we are," said Alex hastily.

At first glance Mog's house looked very grand. Wide steps led up to its huge front door, which was sheltered by a stone hood and flanked by tall pillars. On either side of this was a pattern of oblong, multi-paned windows with a double row of smaller windows above. Somehow everything balanced. You could imagine a coach and six pulling up in front of it—until you noticed that the paint was peeling and the stonework cracked in places. At the top of the steps, too, on one side of the front door, was a bell-push for each of the five tenants who now lived there. It was a house that had come down in the world. Nowadays all that pulled up in front of it was the occasional mini-cab.

Before we were through the front gate Mog had seen us. She was leaning from an upstairs window.

"Come on up," she called. "The front door's open. So's the door to our flat."

"Anyone like to guess what Mog's mum will be doing?" grinned Alex, as we climbed the stairs.

"Good morning, gentlemen," said Mrs Catley in her

soft, drowsy voice. Had she moved at all from the last time we'd seen her? The weight of the sunlight through the vast windows seemed to pin her to the sofa. Or maybe it was the weight of her chinese-silk dressing-gown.

"Good morning, Mrs Catley," we said.

She pointed at the kitchen, lifting her hand so slowly you felt she really needed both hands to do it.

"Katharine's in the kitchen doing the breakfast things. She'll be with you in a minute."

"I'm already here, Mum," said Mog. "It's all finished."

"And what will you be doing today, my darling?"

"I'm going out with Lenny and Alex and Genius. I'm going to show them what a quarter of a million pounds looks like."

"That'll be nice," yawned Mrs Catley.

It was a long, weary yawn but her mouth was still only half as wide as any of ours. Lenny found his voice first.

"What? What did you say you were going to show us?"

"I said I'm going to show you what two hundred and fifty thousand pounds looks like. If you're interested, that is."

"Interested? I'm fascinated!"

"Fine," smiled Mog.

And she winked.

We wanted to start right away, naturally. Instead Mog made us sit down. This had to be on the floor because apart from Mrs Catley's sofa and some bookshelves there was no other furniture in the room. Her mum hated clutter, Mog once explained. She preferred plenty of space for moving around. This must have been a joke though Mog had said it with a straight face.

"Here's what we need for today's adventure," she announced.

From her back-pocket Mog produced a pen-knife and

a small ball of Blu-Tak—the kind that lets you stick something to a wall without leaving a mark when you take it down. She put both on the floor in front of her, then began rolling up the right leg of her jeans. Wrapped round her shin was a folded length of canvas held in place by a couple of rubber bands.

"See?" she said.

Next she rolled up the left leg of her jeans. Round this shin the rubber bands seemed to be holding some wallpaper.

"See?" Mog repeated. "And that's all I need."

"To do what?" demanded Lenny.

"To show you how easy it is to *steal* a quarter of a million pounds once you know what it looks like."

By now our eyes were nearly as wide as our mouths. Behind us Mrs Catley was still being crushed by the sunlight. She couldn't even be bothered to listen, it seemed.

"Of course, I did have to check some details," Mog went on.

"I'll bet you did," said Lenny. "What's she talking about, Genius?"

I shook my head. "Haven't a clue."

"Let's get going then," said Alex. "I can't wait to get rich."

"Hold on!" Mog chuckled. "We're not actually going to *do* the stealing. I just want to try out a method that I think would work. A sort of dummy-run."

"That's a kind a rehearsal . . . a practice," I explained.

"Get away!" said Lenny. "Really? Well I never! Listen, Brains, just because we're not going in for the scholarship like you, it doesn't mean we're *thick*."

As usual it was Alex who came to my rescue.

"Well *I* didn't know what it meant," he admitted.

"Then you *must* be thick. I suppose you really thought Mog was going to steal a quarter of a million quid, too."

"I did just for a minute."

"You prune! Who do you think we are—The Rectifier?"

That made us all laugh. Except Mrs Catley, of course, who was too busy resting.

"Wouldn't it be great if we were," said Alex. "My dad says he ought to be in the New Year's Honours List, that bloke."

"Or blokes," said Mog. "Some people say there's more than one—that there's a whole gang. One person alone couldn't do it, they reckon. Whichever it is, I think it's dead clever."

"My dad says The Rectifier is a sort of Robin Hood," Alex said.

"So do a lot of people," Lenny sniffed. "According to my dad he's a nutcase. My dad reckons we have to pay too much income-tax in the first place. He reckons The Rectifier should burgle The Inland Revenue and give some of it back."

"But that's daft." I said. "If he did that then everyone would have to pay *more* tax to cover what the Government had lost. Anyway, if dishonest people didn't cheat on their taxes honest people wouldn't have to pay so much. That's what my dad reckons."

"Maybe," said Lenny. "But just about everyone cheats the taxman one way or another—poor people as well as rich. Let The Rectifier try to get his hands on my dad's money, though. He'll get himself duffed up good and proper."

"Does your dad fiddle his taxes then?" I asked.

Straightaway I knew I'd said the wrong thing again. Lenny scowled and went red. He looked just like his father—a huge man who ran a market stall down by the river. I swallowed. Why did I never think before I opened my mouth? Sometimes I wondered if I was as clever as everyone told me.

"In the end Robin Hood himself got duffed up good and proper," said Alex. "Probably that'll happen to The

Rectifier, too. One day he'll be caught by one of his victims and crash-bang-wallop that'll be that.''

"Never," said Mog. "He's too cunning."

"He'll make a mistake sometime," Lenny insisted.

A loud knock at the door silenced us.

"Answer that, darling, will you?" yawned Mrs Catley.

"Who will it be, Mum?"

"Dearest, how should I know? Be a sweetheart and find out. Mummy's so tired."

"Okay."

As quick as a cat in the rain Mog was up and over to the door. Even so, a second and louder knock beat her to it. Someone was in a hurry—or in a very bad mood.

"Hold on," Mog called. "I'm coming. Oh . . . hello."

Something in her voice made us look round. In the doorway stood Howard with Mr Skin behind him.

Howard was grinning like a podgy wolf who's tasted blood. But the look of Mr Skin was far more deadly. He was so still and so silent and so black. He made me think of dark alleys and of what I wouldn't want to meet there. Alex began to whistle softly. This was always a sign he was nervous.

Without a word Howard brushed past Mog and sauntered into the room leaving Mr Skin where he was . . . for the moment.

"Did you come up the stairs on your motorbike, Howard?" Lenny asked. Howard stopped. He hadn't expected to see us. His fat grin faded then returned wider than ever as he clicked his fingers and thrust out a hand towards Mog, palm upwards.

"Rent," he said.

"What?"

"Rent. It's due today. Eighty pounds for the month. Cash on the nail. And my chauffeur and I haven't got all day so hurry up about it." Mog stared at him blankly.

"But we paid it three weeks ago. To that man your

father sent. There's still another week to run before he comes again."

"He won't be coming again," snapped Howard. "I'll be collecting the rent in future. With Mr Skin. Any objections?"

"I don't care who collects it so long as it's on the right day. And that's not till next week."

"Show him the rent book," Lenny suggested.

"That's right. Show me the rent book."

"We don't have a rent book," said Mog, patiently. "You know that. We agreed it with your father when we moved in here. Every fourth Saturday we pay eighty pounds, that's all."

"Correct," sneered Howard, "Today's a fourth Saturday and you can't prove otherwise. So pay up or get out."

"No. Sorry, Howard."

"No?"

Howard glanced round the room as if calculating the value of the furniture. Eighty pounds' worth? Nowhere near I'd have said but I didn't doubt for a second that Mr Skin would have carried off the bookshelves and the sofa plus the books and Mrs Catley if Howard ordered it. The chauffeur loomed in the doorway looking more than ever like a security guard at a funeral. It was Howard's body that had to be guarded, though, and Howard was alive and kicking . . . preferably Mog.

"Don't bother carting the stuff downstairs, Skin," he drawled. "Chuck it out of the window. Our tenants are leaving."

"Stop right there," said Mog. "Or you'll be leaving the same way." Howard took a quick step backwards. Then his eyes glinted craftily.

"Better get rid of her first. Lock her in the bathroom."

"What about Lenny and Alex and Genius, Howard?" Mog asked. "Think they'll just sit around while he's doing it?"

We laughed warily and got to our feet. Surely Mog didn't really expect us to throw Howard out of the window? She was bluffing ... wasn't she? From the look on her face it was hard to tell. Especially it was hard for Howard to tell. No one moved. Howard blinked and began to chew his lip. When I saw him trying to work up another sneer I knew we'd won. Or rather I knew we would have won if Mrs Catley hadn't interrupted.

"For God's sake, what a bore it all is! Give the chubby little cheat his money, Katharine, and let me get some rest."

"But Mum—"

"Fetch the money, Katharine."

Mrs Catley's eyelids fluttered and she clasped at her throat as if there were only a couple of heartbeats between her and an early grave.

"Oh, Mum ..." said Mog.

She turned and left the room. When she came back she had an envelope. Howard smirked and opened it.

"I'd better check it," he said. "If you can't count up to four weeks what hope is there you'll get eighty pounds right?"

He licked a finger and riffled through the notes in a slow, showy way.

"... seventy-seven, seventy-eight, seventy-nine, eighty. That'll do. Good thing your mum's got more sense than you have. See you in four weeks' time ... or thereabouts. Come on, Skin."

Howard turned and swaggered out. Instead of slamming the door of the flat, as we expected, Mr Skin closed it with a gentleness that was much more threatening.

"Phew!" said Alex. "I'll bet you're glad they won't be back for another month."

"Or three weeks," Lenny said.

He was watching Mog. She was still standing in the middle of the room staring in front of her. In the window-bay her mother was staring too but out at the treetops as if nothing at all had happened. To look at, she and Mog were amazingly alike—the same face and hair and eyes with the same lightness and toughness of body. It was as if you were looking at the same person twenty years later. Yet Mog crackled with liveliness while her mum drooped with fatigue. How could two people be so similar and yet so different both at the same time?

"Tell you what," said Alex. "There's one person I can think of who'd find this rent business very interesting."

"Who's that?" Lenny asked.

"Well, with no rent book and payments in cash you can bet Howard's dad isn't declaring this money to the taxman. It's going straight into his own pocket—or Howard's. Now who would be fascinated by that?"

"You mean . . ."

"Exactly," nodded Alex. "The Rectifier. I'll bet Mr Bygrave is just the sort of person The Rectifier would rob . . . if he hasn't robbed him already, of course." A sudden noise made us glance across the room. Mrs Catley was yawning again. The sound seemed to wake Mog up.

"It's adventure-time!" she announced. "Follow me, gang!"

The Museum

By now, probably, you've got some idea of the neighbourhood where we lived. Are you in a bit of a muddle about it though? This wouldn't surprise me because it's a very muddling place. How could so much open space be cramped round its edges by so many different buildings? We once constructed a model of the area for a project at school. It looked like a toy city built by a mad giant who was making it up as he went along. Except that in real life it's only part of a city—part of the biggest city in England. Our area seems to be a hodge-podge of odds and ends taken from all the rest. Where else would you find a hundred yard stretch of river bank which contains a scrap-metal yard and a power station alongside a tiny, elegant hospital that was once a monastery? And further on there's a famous sailing ship—all masts and spars and rigging and bowsprit—which floats in the same concrete sea as huge blocks of flats as if it's been marooned amongst cubic ice-bergs. Yet behind all this the park and the heath begin and these were once the hunting-ground for kings and highwaymen. My dad says it's like living in a vast open-air memory-bank with a traffic problem. But he loves it as much as I do.

So does Mog. You could tell by the look in her eye as she marched towards the park gates.

"Where are we going?" Lenny asked.

"The museum," said Mog.

"The museum? What's in the museum worth a quarter of a million pounds?"

"The full-size paddle-steamer?" Alex suggested. "That must have cost quite a bit."

"Oh, terrific. And Mog's going to show us how it could be stolen, is she? By lasso-ing it and lifting it through a hole in the roof, I suppose. Then we'd get Howard to tow it home for us with his motor bike."

"It's not the paddle-steamer," Mog smiled.

"What then?"

"Wait and see."

"Come on, Mog, tell us."

"Ask Genius."

"Why?" said Lenny. "Have you told him already?"

"No. But I'll bet he's worked it out."

"Have you?"

I frowned and thought about it. Then I nodded.

"I think so."

Lenny and Alex looked at me suspiciously.

"It's a painting," I said.

Mog gave a shout of delight and turned a complete somersault. Lots of kids can do that of course—but not with their hands still in the pockets of their jeans.

"It's got to be a painting," I went on. "Because of what Mog's bringing with her."

"Don't get it," said Alex. "Do you get it, Lenny?"

"Well, he's the one with the high IQ so I'll take his word for it."

"I should if I were you," grinned Mog. "Because he's dead right."

"The Scholarship Boy strikes again," Lenny said.

I tried not to smirk which would have annoyed Lenny even more. Sometimes it seemed to me that Mog and I shared thoughts. We got the same idea at the same speed in the same way. Thank goodness the scholarship was for an all-boys' school. I wouldn't have wanted Mog sitting next to me in the exam-room because just possibly she might have done better than me. For example, I still wasn't sure about her exact plan for today.

"Hey!" Alex exclaimed. "They're following us!"

We didn't have to ask who he meant. On the far side of the heath we saw the tubular steel double-cradle frame of the GL 1000-K2 with its overhead camshaft, its semi-wet multi-plate clutch and its five-speed constant-mesh transmission etcetera, etcetera. It crawled along keeping level with us.

"What do they want?" asked Alex.

"Just trying to give us the heebie-jeebies," said Lenny. "If there were a billion ways of being a bully Howard would still invent a new one. Take no notice."

"No," said Mog. "Let's take a lot of notice. Genius, you get behind me and hold my waist. Alex, you get behind Lenny—as if you were riding pillion on a motor bike. That's right. What we've got to do is to let Howard and Mr Skin know they've been spotted and let them see we couldn't care less. Okay? Off we go then . . . baroom-baroom!"

Mog kick-started her imaginary Honda, slotted it into gear with her right hand and accelerated away with her left. Lenny did the same and we baroom-baroomed towards the park gates with Alex and me tilting our noses in the air just like Howard.

Howard was furious. Even four hundred yards away we could see that. He seemed to be shouting at Mr Skin. We saw the motor bike swerve off the road towards us and pick up speed across the grass.

"He can't do that!" yelped Alex. "That's against the law!"

"He's doing it," Lenny said. "And he's coming this way fast."

With its chauffeur and passenger hunched low, the motor bike roared across a football pitch, scattering the kids who were playing there. A flock of seagulls from the river shrieked and flapped into the air just ahead of it.

"Run!" Alex shouted.

We could hear the snarl of the machine now above our

panting for breath. Sheer panic kept me level with the others. Could we get to the gate first before my legs or lungs or heart gave out? Every instant I expected to be mown down by the ten horse-power stampede our teasing had started.

"Keep going!" gasped Lenny. "Keep going! Keep going!"

A frenzy of engine wiped out his voice and seemed to pitch us headlong through the gates before fading as fast as it came.

Still shuddering, we began to untangle ourselves from each other. It was Alex who first noticed we were short of one complete person.

"Where's Mog?" he asked.

Lenny and I froze.

"Where's Mog?" asked Alex again, his voice rising.

Slowly we got to our feet.

"Let's go back," said Lenny.

We didn't dare look at each other. For a moment we couldn't even move. Through the gates of the park I could see acres and acres of heath where Mog might be lying.

"We'd better find her," Lenny went on. "She might . . . she might be . . ."

"She's not," said Alex. "There she is!"

Mog had entered the park by a side gate further down the south wall. She was strolling towards us, grinning.

"Wotcher team!" she announced.

"What happened?" Lenny and I asked together.

"I ran," said Mog. "Like you did."

"You couldn't have," Lenny said. "You're the best runner of the four of us. You'd have got to the park first."

"Only if I was running in the same direction. But I wasn't. I was running towards the bike."

"Towards the bike?" we echoed.

"Sure. It put him off completely. Howard nearly fell off the pillion-seat when Mr Skin swerved round me!"

"'But suppose he hadn't swerved? Suppose he ran you down all the quicker?'"

"Oh, come on, Genius, use those famous brains. Mr Skin's a chauffeur—it's his job. How could he risk killing a bunch of kids in broad daylight while they're walking across a common? He was just bluffing. To amuse Howard, probably. The only real risk was on the road outside the park . . . which you were busy pelting towards. That was where he just missed you. If he'd hit you there he could've said you were playing 'chicken' or something—seeing who was the last one across. He wouldn't have dared clobber me on the grass."

"You mean it was *us* galloping straight at the danger?" Mog nodded.

"That's right, Alex."

"I feel sick."

And I felt humiliated. Why hadn't I thought of that?

"Mind you," said Mog, "if *Howard* had been driving it would've been different. He's such a mad-bonce he might have murdered us all regardless. Thank goodness twelve-year-olds can't get a driver's licence. Can you just see him? 'Not guilty, my Lord. The machine just went out of control. They were four of my closest friends, my Lord. I'll never forgive myself, sob-sob. I'll have a tomb and a memorial erected for them smack in the middle of the heath, my Lord, even if it does cost a couple of weeks of my pocket-money.'"

"Howard can't be that bad," I protested.

"No?" said Lenny.

Suddenly Mog giggled. Whenever she did this you were reminded she was a girl. Boys giggle too, of course, but with Mog it made you notice her long hair and her shape and . . . well, her prettiness. We were always embarrassed when Mog giggled.

"What's so funny?" Lenny asked.

"I told you," said Mog. "Howard nearly falling off his motor bike. He went like this."

She demonstrated. That made *us* giggle. Soon we were copying her. By the time we were past the Observatory and the statue of the General and the long slope that lead down to the museum itself, we'd each got it perfectly—from Howard's lunge backwards with flailing arms to the look of wild panic in his eyes.

"We could add it to our mime of Howard and Mr Skin on bike-back," Alex suggested.

"And perform it the next time we see them," Lenny said.

Mog frowned.

"Why not?" demanded Lenny. "Serves Howard right, doesn't it? Doesn't it?"

"I suppose it does," Mog sighed. "But never mind Howard now. We've got a bit of daylight robbery to mime . . . two hundred and fifty thousand pounds worth."

"And there it is," she said in the museum, five minutes later.

We stared at the painting. Half of it was sky. Then came an horizon of trees, twin spires and an opening out of oblong, elegant buildings fronting the river. The water was crowded with the sails and oars of a couple of centuries ago.

"It's the Naval College," said Alex.

"Not then. It was the Royal Hospital, then. Look—it says so here." Mog pointed to a small label on the screen where the painting hung. Lenny peered at it and read out the painter's name: Canaletto.

"Sounds like tinned vegetables," he said. "Is it really worth that much?"

"They reckon."

We inspected it doubtfully. Not that we weren't impressed. When you stood back from it the picture was sharp as a snapshot but close up you could see many of the details had been caught with a single brush-stroke. Yet how could it cost as much as eight Rolls Royces or a couple of posh houses overlooking the park or about twice a lifetime's work for my dad? Even Mog didn't seem too sure.

"I think this is the one," she said. "Anyway, the method's the same whatever the picture. Now if we were doing this properly we'd need an exact copy just the same size as the original. Quite easy to get, actually—a skilled forger could work it up from one of the postcards they sell downstairs in the museum shop. Also we'd need glass-cutters, a razor-knife and Blu-Tak...oh, and we'd have bought one of the rolled-up maps from the shop on our way in."

"Why?" asked Alex.

"To hide the painting in when we made our getaway. None of the museum attendants would take a second look at one of them."

"When would we do this?" Lenny objected. "How long would it take?" Mog shrugged.

"With practice, no more than five minutes. And we could do it any time this gallery was almost empty. Right now, for instance."

We looked round and saw Mog was right. At the far end was an attendant but he had his eye on a tourist staring at the figurehead of a lion. Round the tourist's neck was a camera—the attendant was making sure he didn't break the museum rules by using it. Behind us, amongst the model ships in glass cases, there was no one. Mog herself was hidden by the screen with the picture.

Most other kids would have stopped at that. Not Mog, though.

"Watch," she said. "But only out of the corners of your eyes so the attendant won't notice we're up to something. Just be casual. This is where the fun begins."

It's not easy to be casual to order. Alex whistled tunelessly. Lenny bent to do up his shoe-lace. I just stood there about as relaxed as a waxwork. But Mog's movements were as quick and as deft as they always were. First she pulled up her left trouser-leg and with her pen-knife cut the elastic bands that held the wallpaper in place. This she smoothed out on the floor till it was perfectly flat. Next she took out the Blu-Tak, divided it into four lumps and rolled it for sticking. All the time I was wondering where I'd seen that wallpaper pattern before. Suddenly I realised. It was right in front of me . . . covering the screen where the painting hung. And the shape and size of Mog's piece matched perfectly the size and shape of the picture.

"Here goes," Mog said.

Her voice was so normal we all jumped. Because we'd been holding our breath we had expected her to whisper—which would have been much more likely to attract attention, of course. Mog stood up and pressed Blu-Tak on the painting's glass shield, each piece on the inside corner of the frame. Then she spread the wallpaper over the glass. Lenny and Alex and I gaped in astonishment. The painting had vanished. On the screen hung what looked like an empty gilt frame. It was as if we were staring straight through to the wallpaper behind.

"See?" said Mog. "Simple! And sticking up a copy of the painting would be just as easy, though it would take a bit longer to cut out the glass and the real picture. Also you'd have to put the glass back afterwards."

"That's incredible," I said.

"Amazing!" said Alex.

Lenny shook his head in disbelief.

"Then you'd just have to smuggle out your quarter of a million pounds' worth of canvas wrapped up in the map," Mog continued. "Hey, look out! Here's our first victim."

She meant the tourist with the camera. Still watched by the attendant, he came ambling along the gallery. From his short, stubby hair and his ugly shoes I guessed he was American. He peered at a museum guide-book,

40

glancing up now and then to check where he was. At the screen he stopped. You could almost see him thinking "Ah, now for the famous Canaletto".

But where was it?

He frowned. His eyes went from the frame to the guide-book and back again. He bent forward and read the label. When he straightened he looked even more puzzled. He turned over a page then turned back. Were there any other empty frames in the gallery? No . . . this was the only one. Probably the painting had gone to be cleaned or was on show somewhere else. But in that case why leave the frame behind? We watched, fascinated, as he tried to work it out.

Eventually he shrugged and gave up. On his way out he paused by the attendant.

"Pardon me for asking, but where's the view ·by Canaletto?"

The attendant's sharp bristly voice came from beneath a sharp, bristly moustache.

"Just down on the waterfront, sir—go through the foot-tunnel to the far side of the river and look back. You'll find the scene much as it was painted two centuries ago."

"Excuse me but I know that. It's the painting itself I want to see. Where is it?"

"You've just been looking at it, sir."

"I haven't. It's not there."

The attendant coughed.

"Come with me, sir. I'll show you."

"Thank you kindly."

Like a parade-ground sergeant-major the attendant stepped smartly along the gallery. At the screen he swivelled to face the American and half-saluted in the direction of the picture.

"There, sir."

"Where?"

"There," snapped the attendant.

"Wallpaper with a frame round it?" asked the American.

At this the attendant almost swallowed his whiskers.

"That might be your opinion, sir. No doubt you've got bigger and better on your side of the Atlantic. But in my view it's a masterpiece! A masterpiece, sir."

"Please yourself, fella," shrugged the tourist. "In my view it's just wallpaper."

Still at attention the attendant watched the American leave. He was too furious even to notice us.

"Wallpaper?" he declared. "A work of genius—just wallpaper?" He half-turned to the screen. On his face was a look of sickly admiration for what he expected to be there. Only it wasn't there. The bunch of keys he had in his hand clattered to the floor.

"Do you want to know where the painting is?" asked Mog sweetly.

The attendant jumped as if he'd been stung.

"Where is it?" he rasped.

"Still in the frame," said Mog.

"Where is it?" repeated the attendant.

"I told you. Have another look—a closer look."

But it was we who got the closer look. Somehow he knew we were to blame. Beneath his peaked cap his eyes glinted as he summed us up. He was about to speak again when he noticed Mog's trouser-leg. It was half rolled up her shin so he could see the elastic bands holding the tight roll of canvas she'd used to represent a fake painting. His breath hissed through his teeth.

"You cunning young . . ."

He sprang forward and grabbed Mog's wrist.

"It's no use trying to get away!" he snarled.

"I'm not trying to get away," said Mog.

"What? Good—you've decided to be sensible, have you? Well, it's no use your gang trying to get away. I'm not letting go of you and I've got a full description of them."

"They're not trying to get away either," Mog pointed out.

"Ah . . . then you'd all better come along quietly."

"Where to?" Lenny asked.

"I'll tell you where to. You, my lad, are for it. All of you. I, personally, am taking you to see—"

"The Curator of the museum," said Mog.

"—the Curator of the . . . exactly! That's exactly who I'm taking you to see. And he'll be calling the *police*."

With a snort of triumph the attendant swung on his heel still clutching Mog's arm.

"Don't forget your keys," she reminded him. "They're still on the floor."

He led us through the long, cool rooms of the museum, each of them sea-green or maritime-blue. We passed galleons and schooners, tug boats and submarines, some of them no bigger than a toy, others nearly full-size. Here and there were uniforms or equipment or weapons, and everywhere diagrams and pictures—of storms and sea-battles and sailors, most of them looking famous. My brain hazy with admirals, I had to trot to keep up. Had Mog gone too far this time? Suppose the Curator did send for the police? Did they allow kids with a criminal record to enter for scholarships? Or was it just possible that Mog was still in control of things?

Suddenly, our attendant halted.

"We're here," he said.

Here was a plain oak door labelled SIR EDWIN FITZLYON: CURATOR. With his free hand Mog's warder straightened his cap and smoothed his jacket. I half expected him to shine his toe-caps on the backs of his trousers like we pretended to do before we went in to see our head-teacher. Instead, he knocked on the door.

"Come in," called a voice.

"You first," said the attendant to Mog. "And you lot next."

This room was bone-white including the carpet. What you could see of it, that is. The clutter of paintings, books, maps and nautical objects made me think of Davy Jones's locker. But neither of the two men there looked much like Davy Jones. One was sitting in an armchair by a bright coal-fire. The other, a gaunt, grey-haired man, was at a desk.

"What is it, Mr Carson?" he said. "Visitors?"

"In a manner of speaking, yes Sir Edwin. Very expensive visitors. This little beggar is a thief, sir. These other three are accomplices. Caught them in the act, sir, practically."

"Really? And what did they steal? Postcards?"

"The Canaletto, sir."

"The . . . the Canaletto?"

"Yes, sir."

For a moment about as long as an ice-age no one moved and no one spoke. Behind the Curator was a window with a view of the Park. On the hilltop I could see the General and the old Observatory outlined against the sky. If only we'd stayed up there.

At last Sir Edwin spoke.

"I take it, Mr Carson—since you've come straight to me without raising the alarm—that the painting has been recovered."

"I know just where it is, sir."

"Pity. A thoroughly boring piece of work. Personally I'd have preferred the insurance money. Where's the painting now?"

"Right here in this very room, sir."

"I beg your pardon?"

"You'll find the painting, sir, attached to the lower part of this little madam's left leg."

"You astound me," said Sir Edwin.

With his lips he was still smiling but the smile had gone out of his eyes. The man in the armchair hadn't smiled since we entered the room. He was as fat as the

Curator was thin and beneath his crinkly slicked-down hair he had a face like a battered toby-jug. His clothes looked expensive but he spoiled their effect by bulging out of them at neck and waist. Where had I seen him before?

"Search her," he said harshly.

"Hardly necessary if Mr Carson is right. Perhaps you'll be kind enough to show us, my dear."

"A pleasure," said Mog, reaching down.

"There!" exclaimed the attendant. "See?"

As soon as Mog had snipped the bands with her pen-knife, he snatched at the canvas and held it up.

"Shall I unravel it, sir?"

"Perhaps you'd better, Mr Carson."

"Shouldn't that be left to an expert?" the fat man interrupted. "The painting's still valuable whatever you think of it, Fitzlyon. He might cause even more damage."

"I hardly think so," said Sir Edwin. "Go ahead, Mr Carson."

"Certainly, sir."

Smugly, like a herald about to make a Royal Proclamation, Mr Carson rolled open the canvas. Now I knew why he'd rushed us past all the other attendants without a word and without so much as a glance at an alarm-bell. He wanted all the credit for himself.

"It's blank," the fat man said.

"What?"

"As I expected it would be," said Sir Edwin. "A joke has been played on you, Mr Carson. At least I hope it's a joke. Where is the Canaletto, my dear?"

"It's where I told him." Mog grinned. "It was never gone in the first place. The trick is to make people think it's gone. All he's got to do is to unstick from the glass four bits of Blu-Tak and a rectangle of wallpaper that matches the screen behind the painting. Then—Hey Presto!—the Canaletto is back." Mr Carson spluttered with fury.

"I'll give you Hey Presto you little minx, I'll—"

"Leave her alone," said the Curator sharply. "I suggest you return to your gallery and do as she says. And next time you suspect this museum has suffered a theft be so kind as to sound the alarm immediately and summon colleagues to your assistance as you have been instructed. Follow the procedures and I shan't mind you looking a fool."

"But sir—"

"I believe I have made myself clear."

"Yes sir, but—"

"Good morning, Mr Carson."

The attendant swallowed hard.

"Good morning, Sir Edwin."

Before the door had closed, the Curator was smiling again. But still not with his eyes. Had Mog noticed this? He leant back in his chair and put his finger-tips together. His hands were broad and stubby—quite unlike the bonyness of the rest of him.

"A neat trick, my dear. Now perhaps you'll be good enough to explain to me what you think the point of it is. So far as I know it's not April the first." Mog noticed now all right. She bit her lip and said nothing.

"To show up my staff, maybe?"

The fat man chuckled nastily.

"She certainly managed to do that, Fitzlyon."

"So she did. It will be some time before Mr Carson gets over it. Is that what you wanted, young lady?"

Poor Mog. Anger from a grown-up never bothered her. She could handle that. It was this gentle approach she found deadly. The Curator was a clever man.

"I beg your pardon? Will you speak a little louder, please?" he asked.

"I didn't . . . I didn't mean to upset him."

"Then what did you mean to do?"

His voice was soft. About as soft as the first touch of a noose.

"I was just . . . practising," said Mog. "I was practising what I might have to do when I take over . . . when I take over from . . ."

"From whom?"

Mog took a deep breath.

"From The Rectifier."

"Ah . . ." said Sir Edwin. "You see yourself as The Rectifier's apprentice?" He didn't seem in the least surprised. The rest of us were astonished. Especially the fat man who glared at Mog as if she'd sprouted horns and a tail like Satan.

"The Rectifier!" he growled. "That self-appointed, interfering do-gooder. Does he realise the taxes we so-called rich people have to pay? Him and his 'collected for the Government by The Rectifier'—who has he collected it *from*, may I ask? From people who've had to risk their money and work themselves skinny for every little thing they've got! And what does the Government do with all these tax contributions anyway? It doles them out to bone-idle good-for-nothings who haven't done a hard day's work in their lives. Yet this Rectifier, whoever he is, gets himself treated like a hero by some people. It's enough to make me vomit!" He bent forward in the armchair, but not to be sick, just to get closer to Mog. "You listen to me, young lady. If it wasn't for 'rich' people there wouldn't even be this museum where you can train to be his apprentice. Most of the money for it came as a gift from a great ship-builder—a millionaire. Did you know that? Without him it wouldn't be here. Isn't that right, Curator?"

"He was certainly most generous," Sir Edwin agreed. "So far as I can recall, though, he didn't finance the museum from unpaid taxes and I believe it's in these that The Rectifier specialises. However, that's hardly our concern right at this moment. Shall we proceed with the matter in hand?" Without waiting for a reply he turned

48

back to Mog. "So you'd like to be The Rectifier, my dear?"

"Yes."

"You and several million other young people, I imagine . . . though not many of them will have made as good a start as you have. How old are you—thirteen, fourteen?"

"Twelve."

"Twelve! An even better start than I thought. There can't be many twelve-year-olds who've spirited away a Canaletto from under the nose of an experienced museum attendant. Or at least appeared to do so. My congratulations . . . and a word of advice. It may help you in your future career. Learn one lesson that—so far as we know—has kept The Rectifier safe: don't try to repeat a success. Because the second time round you'll be expected. Do I make myself plain?"

"Yes, sir."

"Allow me to be quite sure I'm understood. Are you listening? Excellent. So far as I am concerned that is the *first* and the *last* trick you will play in this museum. However tempting, there will be no next time. None whatever. Your apprenticeship will continue elsewhere, my dear. That is all." I tugged at my collar. He'd been talking to Mog but the noose had tightened round all our throats. The Curator wasn't just a clever man, he was a tough one too.

"Is that all you're going to do?" the fat man said.

Sir Edwin lifted an eyebrow.

"That's all I need to do. What more do you suggest?"

A coal shifted in the fire-place. The fat man glanced down at it as though he were considering whether we should be branded. Or maybe clapped in irons, given thirty lashes then keel-hauled and hung up in the museum as exhibits. Why had Mog's mention of The Rectifier made him so furious? Eventually he shrugged. It was like the wobble of a vast blancmange.

"You're the boss," he scowled. "I just supply the money."

"Amongst others," said Sir Edwin. "Including the Government—from tax contributions."

He reached forward and picked up the 'phone on his desk. The four of us stiffened. The Curator smiled. This time his eyes were included.

"Just testing . . ." he said. "I think I've made my point. But should this happen again then I will be making a call. To the police. Is that clear?" We nodded. To our relief he put the receiver down.

"Excellent. Do visit the museum anytime—provided the training programme for your future occupation doesn't involve tampering with what's on show. And perhaps you'll be kind enough, my dear, to collect your four pieces of Blu-Tak and your rectangle of wallpaper from Mr Carson. We have no further use for them. Good morning to you."

"Good morning," we said. "Sir."

Leaving the museum wasn't a comfortable experience. Every attendant seemed to be on the look-out for us. I hadn't realised there were so many. As we trailed through the galleries we felt their eyes on us, some of them angry and all of them curious. A few seemed to be laughing though they did their best to hide it. Mr Carson told us that he had already put the wallpaper and the Blu-Tak in the incinerator. From the way he said it he'd have enjoyed putting us in the same place. We didn't talk to each other until we were back in the avenue that led up through the park.

"Phew!" said Alex. "I thought we were going to end up walking the plank."

He pushed his shaggy, black hair out of his eyes.

"In fact if that fat man had had his way we would've been," he went on.

"Mr Carson wasn't too keen on us, either," I said.

"Us?" said Lenny. "Mog, you mean. We weren't

exactly co-stars, were we? It was Mog's circus, really. We were just also-rans. When we were in that Sir Edwin's room it was only Mog who said a word."

"That's true," agreed Mog. "But I couldn't have done it without you. I wouldn't have had the nerve."

"You couldn't have been as scared as I was," said Alex. "My knees were knocking together so loudly I thought they'd got death-watch beetle. How did you feel, Brains?"

"Can't you see the peculiar way I'm walking?" I said. "It's because my knees are *still* knocking together as if they've got death-watch beetle."

"It was enough to scare anybody," said Lenny, "what with one of them all icy and polite and looking half the time as if he was enjoying it and the other one about to erupt any second like a volcano . . . real Gestapo stuff: first one bashes you then the other kisses it better to set you up for the next bash. Charming. Too much of that and you go bonkers."

"I think it's affected me already," said Alex in a quavery voice.

"Yeah, but you were half-bonkers to start with."

"Three-quarters," Alex insisted.

But before he could launch into his Mad Alex the Gibbering Kid routine, Lenny changed the subject.

"Hey, Mog. What was that bit about being apprentice to The Rectifier? You've never told us that before."

"No, I haven't. Perhaps I've never thought of it before. What do you reckon then? Think it's possible?"

For Mog we'd reckon just about anything was possible. By the time she was grown up would there be anything she couldn't do? Even with Sir Edwin she hadn't actually looked *frightened*. Whoever The Rectifier was now, once he must have been a daredevil twelve-year-old just like her.

There was no chance to tell Mog this, though. From behind us came the sound of a car horn. It echoed across

the park as loudly and grandly as a fanfare. We weren't the only kids who turned round.

"Who's that?" Alex said.

Towards us drove a green Rolls Royce no bigger than a stately home. Its chrome and bodywork gleamed as it whispered beneath the trees. Like peasants when the Lord of the Manor comes by we moved to the side of the avenue. The car was almost level with us before we could hear the tip-toe tickover of the engine. To our surprise it came to a stop. The tinted glass of the driver's window slid down. At the wheel sat the fat man with the sunlight glinting on his crinkly hair.

"Come here," he invited. "A word with you."

All of us stepped forward but it was Mog he was addressing.

"Forget it," he said.

"Sorry?"

"Your dreams of becoming The Next Rectifier. Wise up, young miss. He's just a freak, a goody-goody who wants to play Galahad. He won't last. So far he's been lucky with his meddling but you mark my words, he'll come to a bad end. One of these days he'll throttle himself by biting off more than he can chew. Then we'll see his fan-club squawking a different song."

"Maybe you're right," said Mog. "But that's all the more reason for making sure he has a replacement."

"Like you? A girl?" he sneered.

"Why not a girl like me?"

If he had an answer for that we didn't hear it. The Rolls Royce slid forward again while Mog was still speaking. As it glided round the curve of the avenue by the Summer café I noticed the number-plate: HB1.

"What's the matter?" Alex asked.

"I've . . . I've just realised who that man is."

Mog laughed. "Well done, Genius. I was wondering who would recognise him first. That is Howard's dad. Today you met Howard Bygrave Senior."

Quaggy

Next day must have been a bad day for Howard Bygrave Senior. Whenever he picked up a newspaper or switched on the radio or television there was a report about The Rectifier. This time no money or jewellery or paintings had arrived at the Inland Revenue. Just a slim, brown briefcase. Inside were a couple of dozen typewritten sheets and a file of letters. Together they gave details of how for several years a vast property company had rigged its accounts to make sure it handed over only a fraction of the taxes that should have been paid.

At first, I've got to admit, I was disappointed. Nobody was sure how The Rectifier worked but like most kids I had my own ideas. I imagined him at the dead of night blowing open safes with gelignite or twiddling at their combination-locks with long thin fingers until the numbers clicked into place. Or I saw him leaping from a helicopter on to the roof of a penthouse belonging to some millionaire . . . before swooping off daringly with a couple of priceless treasures. In fact I thought of him as a sort of grown-up version of Mog in the museum. What didn't fit the picture I'd built up was the notion of an ordinary, everyday detective following clues and gathering information bit by bit till he'd amassed the kind of evidence there'd been in the briefcase. What was exciting about that? As usual, it was my dad who explained.

"Just think about it," he insisted. "How much money in unpaid taxes is involved in this one operation?"

"Thousands of pounds?"

"Try again."

"Hundreds of thousands?"

"Still not enough—millions, probably. More than the value of everything The Rectifier has handed over to the Government so far."

"As much as that?" I gasped.

"Certainly. Better still, he's put a stop to the people who've been doing the swindling. They're in serious trouble. High and mighty though some of them are, it'll be prison sentences all round sure as eggs are eggs. How can the authorities avoid it? Especially since The Rectifier sent briefcases with copies of everything to a dozen different journalists. No one will be able to hush this up."

I stared at my dad blankly.

"But why would anyone want to hush it up? Apart from the guilty ones, that is." Dad sighed and pushed his peaked cap to the back of his head. He'd just got back from sorting out a special delivery and he looked tired. More and more often these days he remarked that his mailbag didn't get any lighter. I hated it when he said this. It reminded me how much older than Mum he was and how late in life they'd had me. Also it reminded me why they were so anxious for me to do well. On his face now was the sad, crooked smile he always wore when he was about to tell me something that made him ashamed of the world.

"It's hard to explain, son," he said eventually. "You see, some of the men and women involved in this company are important people. It's not just money and freedom they'll be losing but their whole career."

He glanced down at his polished, post office boots.

"They're powerful people. If The Rectifier hadn't forced things out into the open they might still have got away with it especially since ... since some of them are themselves members of the Government. Not all our rulers are honourable, son. Can you understand that?"

"You mean modern Sheriffs of Nottingham?"

"That's right!"

He looked surprised. He always did when I wasn't as shocked as he expected.

"And not everyone agrees about heavy taxation being a good thing, isn't that right Dad? Don't some people say we'd all work harder if we didn't have to pay so much tax? Also they say the Government wastes a lot of the money it gets from taxes anyway. Don't they?"

"That's as maybe," said my dad. "You must make your mind up about that. But people should still pay what it's lawful for them to pay. This property company has been caught cheating and that's that. Good luck to The Rectifier, I say. He can't catch everybody—just those who should be setting us an example. That's what I reckon."

"So do I, Dad," I said hastily.

It set me thinking though. After my dad had gone downstairs I found I couldn't concentrate on my maths work. Instead I began to wonder. Suppose Lenny's father was right after all when he said taxation was just robbery with the law on your side? What if Mr Bygrave's claim were true—that without rich people we wouldn't have museums or palaces or posh schools like the one where I wanted to go? Not that the school would even look at me without a first-rate performance in the entrance-exam, so kindly get on with it Scholarship Boy . . .

I peered at the question again. It read:

> '*If seven maids with seven mops*
> *Could sweep it in half a year,*
> *How many months,*' *the Walrus asked,*
> '*Would six such maids with six such mops,*
> *Take to get it clear?*'

This was one of the easy ones, I knew. Usually I'd have had the answer in a few seconds. I even recognised where the verse came from—Lewis Carroll's *Through The Looking Glass*. But do you think I could get my brain functioning? Each time I tried to turn the words into numbers they changed into pictures instead, pictures that had nothing to do with maids and mops and walruses. The maids became Mrs Catley stretched on her sofa and making a full-time job of a yawn. The mops were replaced by Sir Edwin with his twinkling eyes and sailor's hands. And the Walrus dissolved into a cut-throat smile beneath a crash-helmet: Mr Skin.

Angrily, I shook my head clear and began afresh. Six months was the time it took seven maids plus seven mops to do the sweeping. So if there were only half a dozen of them . . . they'd never get finished at all in weather like today's. Gusts of rain rattled against my bedroom window. Between our terrace and the terrace opposite every backyard was awash. If Noah were a neighbour with the street for his ark he'd be thinking of casting off. Or at least he'd be making a final check on his animals two-by-two—lion-lion, tiger-tiger, monkey-monkey, walrus-walrus. Come on, Genius, concentrate—concentrate. 'How many months?' the Walrus said.

Ten minutes later I was no closer to an answer. My brain was like a television screen with the focus switch jammed in the wrong position. Suppose this happened in the entrance-exam itself? My stomach turned a slow somersault at the thought and I groaned out loud.

"Anything wrong, son?"

"Nothing, Mum," I said hastily. "Everything's fine. It's just this rain. It's so loud on the roof I can hardly hear myself think."

"Why don't you work in the front room? I know it's a bit damp down there but we could put the fire on."

"No, that's all right. I'll be finishing soon anyway."

She looked at me anxiously.

"You're not overdoing it, are you? You mustn't set too much store by going to this school, you know. I mean, your dad and me would be thrilled but we do realise how hard it is to get in, even for a clever boy. You mustn't make yourself ill."

"It's all right, Mum," I said. "Why did you come up, anyway?"

"What? Oh, I nearly forgot. This came through the door for you just now."

From her apron-pocket she took an envelope. The smile on my face as I glanced at it made her smile too.

"Who's it from?" she asked.

"It's an invitation. From . . . from a friend. Mum, can I go out later? Just for an hour or so?"

"In this rain?"

"I can put my duffle coat on. Please, Mum. It'll do me good."

"Well . . . see what your father says."

"Thanks, Mum!"

Since he delivered mail in all weathers himself Dad was bound to agree. In his opinion a little bit of cloud-juice never did anybody any harm. When Mum had gone I examined the message carefully. It had come by hand. On the envelope was my name—my real name, that is, not the nicknames I'm using in this report. The letters had been cut from different magazines and newspapers so they were all shapes and sizes. The invitation was the same. It looked like a ransom note:

> *Meet me between the two tigers after dark.*
> *We have secrets to stash away.*
> The Next Rectifier

I glanced at my watch. There was almost an hour till dusk and less than a mile to the meeting-place. No cause for hurrying . . . except to stop my heart beating so fast. How was I to pass the time till our rendez-vous? With a Walrus, perhaps?

If seven maids with seven mops took six months, then in one month they'd do 1/6 of the job, each of them contributing 1/42 part of it. So six maids would complete 6/42 of the job in a month. Hence they'd need seven months to finish the task altogether. Simple.

I wrote down the answer—seven months—not bothering with any working out. The problems in the rest of the exercise got trickier and trickier and more and more fun. In a quarter of an hour I'd done them all. Had I been waiting all along to be inspired by The Next Rectifier?

She was standing on a traffic island in the middle of the road. On her head was a shiny black rain-hat that hid her face. Also she wore a matching cape that reached nearly to her ankles. Under the neon lights of the road junction with the rain bouncing ankle-high all round her, she certainly looked mysterious enough to be The Next Rectifier.

"Hello, Genius," she greeted me. "You worked out the clue, then?" She nodded to right and left. On one side of us, still shuttered up before opening time, was a craggy Victorian pub—The Old Tiger. On the other side, just as cluttered with windows-sills and plaster-work was another Victorian pub—The New Tiger.

"I knew where you meant straightaway," I said. "Where are the others?"

"No others. We're on our own for this."

"We're leaving out Lenny and Alex?"

"That's right. They wouldn't take it seriously. This has got to be confidential—till I tell you otherwise."

"Okay, Mog."

Should I have been flattered or frightened? I wasn't sure. As usual I had to trust Mog.

We crossed to the pavement by The New Tiger and began to walk back the way I'd come. It was wet and it was Sunday so the streets were as dead as they ever are in a city. Nothing moved, apart from the rain and the two of us and the splashing past of an occasional car. Suddenly—so suddenly she almost left me behind—Mog darted into a alleyway. I squelched after her. We were in a cobbled yard bounded by the rear entrances of shops and warehouses.

"Is this where we're stashing away the secrets?" I asked.

"Near here," answered Mog.

"Real secrets?"

Mog shrugged.

"Does it matter?"

It mattered to me. With Mog even a dummy-run could be terrifying. Look what happened in the museum! Suppose now, Rectifier-like, she'd got hold of something truly important?

"Don't look so worried, Genius!"

Her chuckle made me feel better. She sounded like a twelve-year-old kid again, not the Master Spy I'd begun to build up in my imagination. Sometimes it seemed to me my mum might be right when she said I had too much imagination for my own good. Or was it Lenny who was right? To Lenny I was just a scaredycat.

"Over there."

Mog was pointing at a long, low wall which seemed to be holding off a different, sunken darkness.

"The Quaggy?"

"Right—a smashing hiding-place. You can't get down to it very easily and what's there, anyway? Just rubbish and running water."

And rats and disease according to most of the people I knew. All my life I'd been told to keep away from the Quaggy. In summer it stank and the rest of the year it had just enough water to conceal the slime and the junk. Once in a while it reminded everyone it was there by becoming a real river and flooding its banks. Then for years it would be half-forgotten—an odd, gurgling canyon that wound round the backs of houses, vanished into tunnels, then appeared again quite suddenly where you least expected it.

"Can *we* get down to it very easily?" I asked.

"No trouble at all. There's a gap in the brickwork near here. And a sort of ramp that leads up from the river-bed. It's for the workmen who have to clear out the really big stuff that gets dumped, I suppose. Anyway it's good enough for us."

"How will we see where we're going?"

"Night vision. Our eyes'll get used to the dark pretty soon. And I've brought a torch for an emergency."

An emergency? What kind of an emergency? It was as if a ghost had tickled me between the shoulder-blades with icy fingers. My voice cracked when I tried to speak and I had to turn it into a cough.

"But what is it we're here to hide?"

"These," said Mog. "I've wrapped them in plastic to keep them dry."

"Books? Are they worth hiding?"

"What do you think? Didn't you get today's news about The Rectifier, Genius? What's written on paper can be used in evidence. It can bring years of swindling to an end. Use your imagination."

My imagination was the last thing I wanted to use. I was frightened enough with not being able to see where I was going. Mog sidled through the gap in the wall and down the ramp like an expert night prowler. I stumbled after her more like a tone-deaf Orpheus blundering into the underworld. Where the slope met the river-bed we paused. Mog laid a hand on my arm.

"What's that?" she whispered.

"What's what?" I squawked.

"Listen a moment. I thought I heard something."

I listened all right. If I'd listened any harder my eardrums would have burst from the strain. I could hear nothing but the hiss of the rain on the river. All round us I could sense the Quaggy . . . and, gradually, something else.

"It's nothing," said Mog. "I'm just getting jumpy."

So why was she still whispering?

We picked our way over stones we could only feel and through water we could only hear. And slowly, so slowly I hardly knew it was happening, our eyes did adjust to the dark. To the left was the black shape of a tree hanging low over the river. To the right, a black building soared up into a black sky. Ahead was a black tunnel. Was this where we were going?

"Wait," murmured Mog suddenly.

"Why? What is it, Mog?"

"Quiet. Keep still."

We were so still and so quiet everything round us seemed more alive than we did. Again I could hear nothing I didn't expect to hear. Except, that is, for... for what? Was there... could there be... something, or someone, lying in wait?

If so, it was done well enough to fool Mog. After a long moment she moved forward into the mouth of the tunnel. Here she switched on the torch. In its beam we saw an arch of mossy brickwork, stretching away from us to the limit of the torchlight. From the roof hung clusters of cobwebby plants or plant-like cobwebs that trailed down almost to the water.

"How far in do we go?" I asked.

"Till we get there," Mog said.

Her voice echoed slightly.

"Yes, but where's *there*?"

"We'll know it when we see it. All we need is a place to stow away these books. It's got to be dry and it's got to be easy for us to come back to but difficult for anyone else to find even if they're looking for it."

"We could put them anywhere then," I suggested. "Who would think of the Quaggy as a hide-out for books?"

"Maybe plenty of people. The person who watched us come in here for a start."

"Who?" I yelped.

"Didn't you see him, Genius? If he's still where he

was, then we crept right beneath him. He was staring over the parapet."

Just in time my breathing and my heartbeat resumed more or less normal service.

"Who was he?" I asked. "Did you recognise him? Did—did he recognise us?"

Mog shrugged. "No point in panic even if he did. He hasn't followed us at any rate. Look." She switched off the torch. Behind us the tunnel entrance framed a more delicate, open-air darkness as if the night shadows outside had been faded by the rain. No-one was there.

"Come on," said Mog. "Forget him. He was just a passer-by, probably. He saw less of us than we did of him, I reckon."

The further we went into the tunnel the more I wanted to hold my nose. The smell was a blend of cats and stale air and rotting brickwork. Every so often something brushed my face as if the stink had solidified into a wispy, clinging nastiness. It made me feel sick. I followed Mog and the torchlight only because I was frightened of being left behind. Ahead of us the tunnel curved into pitch black.

"Hey!" Mog announced suddenly. "This is it."

She pointed at the tunnel wall. About shoulder-high there was a stretch of loose bricks.

"Help me get them out."

"Won't that weaken the structure?"

"I think we can take a chance on that, don't you?"

Mog flashed the torch around us. I had to admit there were a lot of bricks.

"You hold the books and the light. I'll clear a hiding-place. Genius, don't look so nervous. I promise I won't bring the roof down."

I chuckled to indicate that no-one in his right mind could think such a thing. While Mog made the hole, though, I kept an ear cocked for the first sound of collapse.

"Can you stop fidgeting?" Mog asked.

"Sorry."

It was trembling not fidgeting. I gripped the torch more tightly.

"Nearly there, I reckon. The bricks are shifting so easily you'd think it's been used before—a sort of wall-safe in a sort of vault. Let's try the books for size. No . . . not quite big enough."

"Try them the other way round. Smooth down the plastic."

"That's it! Well done, Genius. Now, I'll just replace the bricks at the front of the hole and we're finished . . . There. Is that all right?"

"Looks the same as before."

"Smashing. Let me get rid of these left-over bricks, though, or someone might spot where they've come from."

"Who?" I asked. "We must be the first people who've been in here for years."

"You never know," said Mog.

The spare bricks rattled and splashed in the darkness as she tossed them away. As soon as I'd given her back the torch she switched it off.

"Don't want to attract attention as we leave," she explained.

But we'd already attracted attention. From beyond the bend in the tunnel, magnified by its echo, came a snatch of mean laughter. It was followed by the sound of an engine: about a thousand ccs of engine.

"It can't be!" I gasped.

"It is," Mog said grimly. "Mr Skin and the Bully-Bike."

I heard her clawing at the brickwork to retrieve the package.

"Leave it, Mog!"

"No. It won't take a moment. The bricks seem to have jammed. I must've packed them in too tightly."

"Leave it—please, Mog! There's no time. He's coming. You're too far over, anyway. That wasn't where—"

"Yes it was," Mog said. "I'm nearly there."

The growl and splash of the motor bike masked the clatter of bricks and the rustle of plastic. Already the beam of its headlight probed our curve of the tunnel.

"Quick, Mog. He's almost here," I begged.

"Got it! Okay—run for it, Genius!"

As near full-pelt as the Quaggy allowed us, we scrambled for the mouth of the tunnel. We reached the ramp neck-and-neck and were dead level at the gap in the wall before I realised Mog was steering me.

"This way," she hissed. "Into that doorway."

With her fingers locked round my arm I didn't have much choice.

It was the delivery entrance to a warehouse. I slumped in its shadows and struggled to catch my breath. Gasp by gasp I got my lungs under control. Mog scarcely seemed winded. She was peering across the cobbles towards the Quaggy.

"Where is he?" she demanded. "He's taking his time."

"He's bound to catch us up," I groaned, "however long he takes to get through the tunnel."

"Of course he is. That's why I want him ahead of us. As soon as we know which direction he's going in we can go the opposite way."

"If he doesn't see us first."

"He won't, unless we're careless. Here he comes!"

We heard the motor bike roar from the tunnel and make a skidding turn across stones and junk and water. With its engine snarling it mounted the ramp. For a brief moment at the top it seemed to hover, its headlight splitting the darkness, before its wheels bounced on cobbles and it was gone. Its noise trailed into the night.

"Time for us to vamoose too," said Mog. "Keep your eyes . . . er . . . skinned."

"Very funny."

All the way home I expected to be ambushed. Mog led me via alleyways, yards, fences and back gardens that I never knew existed though I'd lived in the area years longer than she had. No one, not even Mr Skin, could have followed us—unless he was able to read minds or fly. The trouble was I half believed he could do both. For how had he spotted us in the first place?

"Fluke," said Mog. "But why chase us down the Quaggy? Howard wasn't even with him."

"He's probably had orders to molest us every chance he gets," I said bitterly. "You know what Howard's like. He hates your guts, Mog. Look what he did with that catapult when you were on the bridge. He only just missed killing you." Mog shook her head.

"Now that *was* a fluke. Howard was lucky to hit the bridge let alone me."

"Maybe he'll get even luckier next time."

"Don't be so morbid."

"Well he's had three attempts this week, hasn't he?"

"Three?"

"The catapult, plus two tries at running us down with the motor bike."

"Genius, you truly do *exaggerate*. Outside the park they were just trying to scare us. And this time . . . well, there was something funny about about this time." Mog must have meant funny-peculiar. There certainly wasn't anything funny-ha-ha about what had happened in the Quaggy. I could still hear the rasp of laughter and the throb of Howard's K2 flat-four four-stroke looming behind us as we fled from the tunnel.

"We didn't finish the job either," Mog said. "We've still got our secrets to hide."

From under her cape she produced the plastic bag.

"Why didn't you leave it there?" I asked.

"Because I'm daft, I suppose. I'd had the feeling we were being watched all along but somehow when I knew who it was I got furious. I wasn't going to leave anything for *him*."

"Not even a couple of old books?"

"All of a sudden it felt like more than that. It felt like I'd be giving up. That doesn't make sense, I know, but what would The Rectifier have done? Suppose these were the results of a whole investigation like those files that have just been sent to the Inland Revenue and the newspapers. Would *he* have abandoned them? Of course not. Can't you see that?"

"Mog," I said. "You truly do *exaggerate*."

She gave such a shout of laughter I almost clapped my hand over her mouth in case Mr Skin was within earshot. Mog was the only kid I knew who really enjoyed a joke against herself.

She was still giggling when we reached her street. The rain had stopped and the whole sky was on the move. Right now there was an interval of moonlight which made her house look grander than ever. On the steps Mog paused.

"You will still help me, Genius, won't you? Next time, I mean."

"Sure," I said.

"Because there's got to be a next time. You do realise that, don't you? My mum says I've got to start young if I'm going to be The Next Rectifier." My heart sank several fathoms into my stomach.

"Sure," I said again.

Mog beamed.

"I knew I could rely on you. Here—look after the books till we've thought of somewhere. It's got to be somewhere special . . . somewhere that makes the Quaggy seem *obvious*."

"Sure," I croaked. "Thanks."

"Keep them safe, Genius. And keep them secret. See you."

"See you, Mog."

I crossed the heath with the plastic bag under my duffle coat. Never has a parcel been carried more cautiously. I treated it as if it were bomb-shaped and had started ticking. Somehow I knew that Mr Skin would still be looking for us. Just as I knew, somehow, that for Mog these were more than just books and it was more than just a game.

A Lesson With Mr Skin

Old books in a dirty plastic bag—that's all the parcel was. Yet I hoarded it like some rare treasure. It was hidden under a floorboard beneath my bed. Even my mother couldn't have found it and she spring-cleaned my room daily. The parcel was as safe and as secret as Mog could have wished. Till she'd found a place of her own, that is.

Why did I make so much fuss about something so worthless, you may ask? What made me play along with her?

I'm not sure. Perhaps it was the same reason Mog chose me for a helper in the first place and not Alex or Lenny: Mog and I were both mad. I don't mean we were foaming at the mouth or thought we were Napoleon. I mean we were both *seeing* things ... things we wanted more than anything else in the world. With me it was a scholarship, leading to a straw hat and a posh school uniform. With Mog it was a build-up of guts and gumption to be followed by a lifetime of adventure. The two of us dreamed of a future we knew would come only if we worked for it hard enough. What we both needed was proper *training*. So when Howard made his free offer I wasn't surprised that Mog alone understood why I had to accept it.

"Extra lessons?" Alex exclaimed. "With Howard's private tutor? And without it costing you a penny? When did he ask you?"

"This morning at breaktime."

"Never mind when," said Lenny. "The question is— why? What's the catch?"

"There's no catch. All I do is join in with Howard's lessons. He reckons his tutor suggested it. He says someone who's working for the same scholarship will give Howard a bit of competition. It'll spur him on—a final tune-up for the exam itself."

Alex shook his head doubtfully.

"You sure that's all? Knowing Howard, I'll bet he's got something else up his sleeve. Why is he going in for the scholarship anyway? His dad could *pay* for him to go there. Come to think of it, Howard's dad could probably afford to buy the whole blinkin' school. He already seems to own a chunk of the museum."

"Don't forget they're bigheads," Lenny pointed out. "And remember they're potty about money. If Howard wins a scholarship it'll save his dad thousands of quid and give them something to swank about, too. Howard's bad enough now, arriving every day on his chauffeur-driven motorbike. Imagine what he'd be like then! He'd probably parachute into the playground from his own private 'plane."

"I see what you mean," said Alex. "With the pilot using a vapour-trail to write *Well done, Howard* in the sky!"

"Exactly. Of course, Brains told Howard to get knotted."

I swallowed and said nothing. Lenny looked at me suspiciously.

"Didn't you?"

"No."

"You didn't? You mean you accepted?"

Both boys stared at me in astonishment.

"Why shouldn't he accept?" asked Mog. "After all, the lessons will do Genius far more good than they will Howard. You've heard what Miss Garner says—she hasn't got time to teach Howard and Genius specially, what with getting all the rest of us ready for the High School. This way they'll both get the same chance."

"But don't you see, Mog?" protested Lenny. "It'll be breaking up the gang!"

"Breaking up the gang? Just because he'll be spending a couple of hours a week in Bygrave Palace? How d'you work that out? More like strengthening the gang, I reckon. We'll have a spy in enemy headquarters."

"That's true," said Alex. "I hadn't thought of that. Neither had you, Lenny."

"Maybe I hadn't. But I still don't like it. And maybe your mum and dad won't like it either—taking charity from that fat snob."

"They've left it up to me to decide. I asked them at lunchtime."

"Well, that settles it then." Lenny sniffed. "Don't forget to wipe your boots before you tread on the mink carpet. How will you get home afterwards? Piggy-back from Mr Skin or a quick trip across the heath in the Rolls?"

"I've got to make my own way there and back."

"Really? One foot in front of the other like everybody else? Poor old Scholarship Boy."

"Leave off," said Alex. "It's not that bad. And like Mog says, who knows what he'll find out? When do you start, Genius?"

I licked my lips, They wouldn't like this bit either.

"Now."

"Now? You mean right now? Today?"

"I'm due at Howard's in twenty minutes."

"I see. Doesn't waste any time, does he?"

"Let's not hold them up," Lenny said. "Think of all that brain-power going to waste. Come on, Alex. Coming, Mog?"

"I'll catch you up."

"There's no need to wait, Mog," I said miserably.

She waited anyway. Lenny and Alex didn't even say goodbye to me.

"Cheer up, Genius. They'll get over it. In a way I

wish I was coming myself. I'd like to see Howard's famous mansion—with its gold-leaf wallpaper and fur-lined lavatory seats! Or so they say. You'll keep your eyes open, won't you?"

"Why?"

"Evidence, of course. For The Rectifier. See you later, Genius."

"Thanks, Mog. See you later."

She winked then turned and ran after the others. I had no idea what evidence she meant but for Mog I'd have memorised every blade of grass on the Bygrave Estate. But why had Howard made this offer? Was his plan to get at Mog through me?

The avenue where Howard lived was so wide you could have played five-a-side football across it. Not that any kids would have dared. They'd have been run over by the Bentleys and Aston-Martins and Lamborghinis. Even the trees here seemed lusher than on our side of the heath. Already they were smudged with greenery and made a dry sound when they rustled like banknotes being counted. Beneath them there was no pavement—only turf and earth. Perhaps people without cars weren't wanted. The sound of my own footsteps made me feel shy.

Every house was set back in a hush of its own. I tried not to stare at them but from the corner of my eye I still caught glimpses . . . of an elegant spiral staircase behind a wall of glass for example. Would I live somewhere like that one day? Or maybe next door where ivy drooped over leaded windows? I didn't care which, really. Each home was different but they were all somehow alike. How was this? I was halfway down the avenue before I'd worked it out: there wasn't a detail here that hadn't been *chosen*. Whatever it was—small as a doorknocker or large as a lily-pond—the owner wanted it that way. That's what it means to be rich.

"Gosh!"

My mouth gaped open when I saw the Bygrave residence. It was the size of a cinema and the shape of a watch-tower. The brickwork was jet-black with long gashes of dark-tinted glass for windows. In front the ground sloped down to a row of garage doors, also black, while a black-tiled bridge sloped up to an entrance of glistening black steel. The house looked half like a strongbox and half like a display case.

"You're here, then," Howard drawled.

I jumped and swung round. He'd been waiting for me, leaning against a tree.

"Hello, Howard."

"You're five minutes early. Want to get your money's worth, do you?"

"Money? I thought I wasn't paying for these lessons?"

"Yes? Oh . . . that's right," said Howard as if he'd just remembered. "Come on then."

Our heels rang on the bridge which seemed to sway gently beneath us. At the top we paused.

"Watch this," Howard said.

He clicked his fingers. With scarcely a whisper the steel door slid aside. Before I could step forward Howard put a hand on my arm.

"Wait. Let it close again."

The door slid back.

"Now you try—do what I did."

I clicked my fingers. Nothing happened.

"Have another go," Howard invited.

It seemed to me I copied Howard exactly but still nothing happened.

"What am I doing wrong?" I asked.

"You're not me," said Howard. "That's what's wrong."

Again he snapped finger and thumb. For him it was like *open-sesame*.

There was magic about the rest of Howard's house, too. It made me think of a castle built a thousand years

in the future—full of tapestries and open stone-work but with sudden outbursts of glass and steel. I wouldn't have been surprised to come across a full suit of armour. I wouldn't have been surprised to come across a complete astronaut's suit, either. Yet it all fitted together. Only Howard looked out of place. Waddling ahead of me, he looked like a frog that would never turn into a prince.

"We'll go down to my rooms," he said. "They overlook the gardens." Rooms? Gardens? Did the Bygrave family have two of everything?

"Here we are," said Howard. "My suite's only got three rooms. When we extend the house I'll have more, naturally. How many rooms do you have?"

"None," I said.

"None? Where do you sleep?"

"I've got a hutch in my dad's backyard. Of course I have to share it with a rabbit. It's not too bad, really, except when people poke lettuce leaves through the wire."

Howard stared at me blankly.

"Oh, I see," he said at last. "You're joking."

I took a deep breath.

"No, I'm not. It's terrific if you like fresh air and don't mind bits of straw sticking in your bum. But you'd hate it, Howard. After all you've got a lot more bum than I have for the straw to stick into."

Lenny couldn't have said it better. Howard looked as if he'd swallowed a stag-beetle. He made a good recovery, though, I have to admit that.

"I've driven down your street," he said. "To me your whole house looks like a rabbit-hutch."

For a split second I had another Lenny-reply on the tip of my tongue. My mouth half opened to say it even if it did finish my private lessons before they'd started. What stopped me was the clothes I saw hanging in the first of Howard's rooms: a posh school uniform with a straw hat. Slowly my mouth shut.

"My outfit," Howard explained. "Got yours yet?"

I shook my head.

"It's tailor-made, of course," he went on. "None of the off-the-peg rubbish you get for the local comprehensive. My dad says State Schools can be fine to start you off. After that you need to find your natural level."

His eyes flicked over me as if he didn't have much doubt about my natural level. With these lessons he was just using me, I could see that, much in the way a stable uses a work-horse to help exercise a thoroughbred. My cheeks burned. From my teeth to my toes I felt myself clenched with fury. I still had time to tell Howard to get lost, stuffed, knotted and take a long walk off a short pier. That's what Lenny would have done.

"So shall we get started?" Howard said.

My voice was so faint I scarcely heard it myself.

"What did you say?"

"I said . . . I said okay. Let's get started."

"Good. Come and meet my tutor . . . I mean *our* tutor."

"He's here already?"

"He lives here," said Howard.

"In the house?"

"Of course he does. I want him available all the time."

You would, I thought.

Howard's rooms made it clear he wanted everything available all the time. He had more books than our school library and more toys and sports equipment than a department store. And that was judging by what I could see. There were closed cupboards, too, with great double-doors from floor to ceiling. What marvels did they contain? The best things in life are free, my mum and dad sometimes say and probably they're right. But the second-best things in life cost money and whatever their price tag Mr Bygrave had stock-piled these for his son. Even the tall windows in each room looked like open-shelves—as if the garden, and the city beyond the garden, and the rest of the world beyond the city were in storage exclusively for Howard. He led me through to the third room.

"My study," he announced. "And *our* tutor."

"Good evening, gentlemen," said the tutor.

"Good evening," said Howard.

My lips made the shape of 'Good evening' but the sound didn't come. The shock was too great. Perhaps I should have guessed who our tutor would be. Perhaps you've guessed already. It was Mr Skin.

"Please sit down, gentlemen," he said in his double-edged voice. We sat down.

He was dressed in his usual black leather but without helmet or gauntlets. For the first time I saw his face. It was as thin and expressionless as his voice—a tailor's dummy of a face, the kind you can't recall the instant you look away. All you'd remember would be those black, glittering eyes. Mr Skin fitted the house perfectly. He was a bogyman from the past and a robot from the future. But what was he doing giving lessons for an entrance-exam?

"With your permission, Master Howard, we'll start with a poem. As part of the test you'll be taking, you're asked to read a passage then answer some questions about it."

"Comprehension," said Howard, "We do that with Miss Garner."

"I'm glad to hear it," said Mr Skin. "The poem I've chosen is in front of you. It's called *Romance* and it's by WJ Turner. Read it silently, please." Determined to outdo each other, Howard and I were so quiet we'd have been deafened by a pin-drop. When I'd read the poem three times I had it by heart:

> *When I was but thirteen or so*
> *I went into a golden land,*
> *Chimborazo, Cotopaxi*
> *Took me by the hand.*

My father died, my brother too,
    They passed like fleeting dreams,
I stood where Popocatapetl
    In the sunlight gleams.

I dimly heard the master's voice
    And boys far off at play,
Chimborazo, Cotopaxi
    Had stolen me away.

I walked in a great golden dream
    To and fro from school—
Shining Popocatapetl
    The dusty streets did rule.

I walked home with a gold, dark boy
    And never a word I'd say,
Chimborazo, Cotopaxi,
    Had taken my speech away:

I gazed entranced upon his face
    Fairer than any flower—
O shining Popocatapetl
    It was thy magic hour:

The houses, people, traffic seemed
    Thin fading dreams by day,
Chimborazo, Cotopaxi
    They had stolen my soul away!

Chimborazo, Cotopaxi and Popocatapetl are volcanoes in Mexico, I knew that. I also knew at once that in the poem it doesn't matter what they are: the names stand for anything, anywhere that's enchanted and special—or seems that way when you're a kid. My own golden land, for example, was closer to home and you reached it only if you won a scholarship.

"Ready?" our tutor asked.

"I'm ready," Howard said. "I don't know about him."

"Me too."

"Good," said Mr Skin. "Before we begin, remember one thing. Discussing a poem is a bit like detective-work. You might need to follow a hunch but you've always got to back up that hunch with evidence. You only persuade other people you're right if you can point to what makes you think and feel that way. Do you understand me?"

We both nodded.

"So . . . some easy questions first."

And easy they were. Was he just warming us up? Did he want to set us talking . . . making up our own comments? Eventually, Howard did.

"He keeps on using the same three words," he remarked, "Chimborazo, Cotopaxi and Popocatapetl."

"Why?"

Howard shrugged.

"Why?" repeated Mr Skin.

"They're magic words," I said.

"Go on."

"They sound magic. Because they come from far away. They crop up over and over again like . . . like a chant, an incantation. It makes the romance of the poem somehow real . . . like . . . like that bit in *Jack and the Beanstalk*—"

Howard gave a hoot of laughter.

"*Jack and the Beanstalk?*" he scoffed. "A fairy story?"

"That's right," I insisted. "That bit where the man who wants the cow asks how many beans make five and Jack says two-in-each-hand-and-one-in-the-mouth. You can sort of feel and taste the beans. It's the same with Chimborazo, Cotopaxi and Popocatapetl—you can sort of feel and taste the golden land. They're how-many-beans-make-five words."

Mr Skin leaned forward. His sharp, dry voice was—for him—almost excited.

"Say something like that in your exam and if the school's got any sense at all it'll hand you a scholarship on the spot."

I felt like blushing and beaming and shouting yippee. Only one thing held me back. He wasn't talking to me. His eyes were on Howard. Howard was the real pupil. I was just a stooge.

The rest of the lesson made it clear that to Mr Skin I didn't matter at all except as a prop to help Howard on his way. We worked at written and spoken English, at maths, and especially at what we should expect during our exam-visit to the school. Ninety minutes went by at the pace of ninety seconds. Yet not for an instant was I allowed to feel I was the centre of attention.

"That'll do for today," he declared, all too soon. "Now, for next time—" He paused and half-turned to the door behind him.

"Come in, Mr Bygrave," he invited.

Neither Howard nor I had heard a sound. A long moment passed. Mr Skin stood up.

"Come in, Mr Bygrave."

He jerked the door open and saluted. From the look on Mr Bygrave's face it was a waste of politeness.

"How's it going?" he demanded.

"He's working well, sir—with much better concentration now he has a partner."

"Will he get the scholarship?"

"It's too soon to say."

Mr Bygrave jabbed a finger into Mr Skin's shoulder.

"Just remember—no scholarship, no bonus. Understood?"

"Perfectly, sir."

"Now come with me . . . I've a special project for you. See your friend out will you, Howard. Tell him he—"

Mr Bygrave broke off. His eyes narrowed as he peered at me.

"Don't I know you from somewhere, lad?"

"I'm in Howard's class at school, sir."

"That all? Haven't I seen you . . ."

"He's never been here before, Dad," Howard interrupted. "He's only here because he's the cleverest boy in the school."

"Except for one, Howard," said Mr Bygrave.

Howard forced a smirk onto his face.

"Except for one, Dad."

"Good. Don't you forget it. Bygraves beat *everybody*. Now come with me, Skin."

To my surprise Howard seemed as relieved as I did when they'd gone. And he seemed in no hurry to get rid of me which was even more surprising. He put his feet up on the desk and leaned back in his chair.

"What do you think of our Mr Skin?" he asked. "As good a tutor as he is a chauffeur?"

"Better, I reckon."

"Yes, he's pretty clued-up. He has to be to work for me and my dad. He'll get me that scholarship all right. You can bank on that. Are you wondering why someone like him does work for my dad and me?"

"Well . . . I suppose I am, yes."

"I'll tell you. Two reasons. First this one."

Howard twiddled fingers and thumb.

"Do you know what that means?"

"Money," I said.

"Correct. We pay him well. But there's another reason too. Would you like to know where Mr Skin was before we gave him a job?"

"Yes, I would."

"I thought you would. He was in prison."

"Prison?" I echoed. "What for?"

He made me wait for an answer. He inspected his fingernails, smoothed down his hair and flicked some imaginary specks of dust from the toe-caps of his shoes.

"Maybe I'd better not tell you," he said finally. "You might be too scared to come back here."

"What was it then,?" I asked, trying to sound casual. "Murder?"

"Murder? Oh no, it wasn't quite murder. You see,

they couldn't prove he'd done it on purpose. So they had to call it . . . manslaughter."

By now Howard was sneering from ear to ear.

"Get the picture?" he went on. "Mr Skin's clever, all right. My dad says he's got enough brains and education to have been a top teacher or a top tycoon or a top just about anything. But he's also greedy which made him *too* clever and he ended up in the clink. That's why he's working for us. That's why he'll do anything . . . anything my dad or I say."

Through the window I could see Mr Bygrave and Mr Skin strolling beneath the trees on a lawn like a wall-to-wall carpet. From his gestures Mr Bygrave seemed to be saying quite a lot. And from the crisp nod he gave now and then Mr Skin seemed about to do as he was told. Whatever the special project was, I shuddered to see them setting it up.

"If he's that good," I asked, "why does Mr Skin spend so much time ferrying you about on a motor bike? Isn't that a waste?"

"It's an investment," said Howard.

"A what?"

"My dad says by investing in me he's investing in the future. That's why I've got to have the best of everything—because I've got to be the best. My dad says there's only one place for a Bygrave and that's on top."

Something in Howard's remark made me glance at him. For a moment I thought I saw tears in his eyes. It must have been a trick of the light.

"I'd better be going," I said. "When's the next lesson?"

"Tomorrow."

"Okay."

"You'll . . . you'll come, then?"

I stared at him in surprise. If he was that frightened I'd say no, why try to scare me with stories about Mr Skin's past history? And he'd scared me rigid.

"What if I refuse? What'll you do—send Mr Skin as a press-gang?"

In a trice his expression changed and he was back to the usual Howard.

"He'd do it if I order him. So don't be late."

"I'll be on time . . . if I come at all. See you, Howard. Maybe." Somehow I kept the quaver out of my voice.

Crossing the bridge back to the avenue I felt as tough and as proud as Lenny again. Well, nearly. Lenny would never have come in the first place. What would happen, I wondered, if I did stay away? Would it affect my chances of a scholarship that much? What could Howard and Mr Skin do—kidnap me? In broad daylight? That was just Bygrave bluster, surely, like the tale about Mr Skin's manslaughter. It couldn't be true. Not here, in real life, amongst these posh, beautiful houses. There was nothing to worry about. So why was I haunted by a vision of a black uniform and black, glittering eyes and the dull throb of a motor bike . . . ?

It was the dull throb of a motor bike that made me turn round. Lounging back in the saddle and steering with one hand, Mr Skin swung onto the road as cool as a cowpoke rounding up a stray calf. I heard myself whimper with panic. How could I uproot my feet? Where could I run? Both questions came too late for an answer. With a sudden revving of engine and a neat swerve Mr Skin-plus-machine blocked my path.

He switched off and lifted his vizor with agonising slowness. Was this the same face he'd had in the house? This skull with a slit for a smile?

"Master Howard says he's sorry to delay you but would you be kind enough to do him a small favour?"

"What favour?" I managed to say.

"He'd like you to deliver a message."

"Can't—can't you deliver it?"

Mr Skin's smile spread wider as he leaned forward.

"He's particularly anxious for you to deliver it. And to bring back any reply when you come for your next lesson. You will be coming for your next lesson, will you?"

I swallowed.

"Okay."

"Excellent. I do very much look forward to seeing you . . . whether there's a reply or not. The message is for your friend Katharine Catley."

"Mog?"

"It's a short message. Easy to remember if you're someone studying for a scholarship. Tell her 'the landlord will collect this month's rent next Saturday'. That's all."

"But you collected it last Saturday!"

"Really? I don't recall that. And I'm sure Master Howard doesn't."

"But I was there! Don't you remember?"

"You were? Then you know already where to take the message. Perhaps you could call in on your way home. Master Howard will be most grateful. And you'll bring back an answer? Tomorrow?"

His gaze seemed to throttle me. Eventually I was able to nod.

"Splendid. How disappointed I'd be if you didn't arrive . . ." The engine roared into life. Before the sound had died away Mr Skin was out of sight.

It was one of those clear, sharp Spring evenings when the trees and the temperature look back to December but the sky looks forward to August. Not that I took much notice of my surroundings. I was lost in a world as remote as Popocatapetl. All the way to Mog's my mind was cluttered with straw hats and manslaughter and the message I had to deliver. The shock of Howard's offer, followed by the shock when I discovered who his tutor was, had left me limp and muddled. But that day had one more shock in store for me. It began as I approached

Mog's house and suddenly saw her. She was perched high in one of the trees that lined the driveway.

From her branch to the ground was a bone-breaking drop of about twenty feet. I sighed. Hadn't I been through all this just a couple of days before? Ah well, at least this time there was no danger from trains or electric rails. The risk here was scarcely a risk at all with Mog's skill. Or so I thought till I realised what she was trying to do. She wasn't perched . . . she was poised. She was poised to leap from the tree to an ornamental balcony that jutted from the house. For a monkey or Tarzan no more than a quick flip through the air was involved. For a girl of twelve the gap looked as wide as the Grand Canyon. She had her back to me but it was clear from her crouch and her stillness that she was on the point of jumping. I held my breath and crossed my fingers so hard my knuckles hurt. At the moment she sprang I closed my eyes. I heard a shudder of branches and a scrabbling on masonry. When I opened my eyes I saw nothing but a window closing. She was inside the house already.

"Mog Catley!" I exclaimed in admiration.

"Not bad, eh?" she replied.

I turned round so fast I almost left my clothes back-to-front.

"Mog!"

"Hello, Genius. Had a good lesson?"

"How did you get here?"

"What d'you mean?"

"From the tree across to the balcony, then downstairs and out again till you came up behind me . . . all in a split second?"

"Genius, what are you drivelling on about? Oh . . . wait a minute. You thought . . . you thought . . ."

Mog's whole face opened up in a gurgle of laughter. With her bright eyes, her freckles and her long tied-back hair she'd have been the prettiest girl I knew if she

86

weren't leader of our gang. Though I had no idea what was so funny I found myself grinning too.

"But how did you do it?" I asked. "Or was it an optical illusion?"

"Genius, can't you guess? Who looks so much like me at a distance you couldn't tell us apart?"

I stopped laughing at once.

"You're not saying . . ."

"Of course I am! That was my mum up in the tree not me. Probably she's forgotten her key again."

"Your *mum* could do that?"

"Well don't look so surprised. It's not that difficult. Often I do it myself. I've told you—Mum teaches me how to do all these things."

"Who taught her?" I asked faintly.

Mog shrugged.

"She's always been able to do them. Anyway, how did the lesson go?"

"It was smashing, Mog. Exactly what I needed. And do you know who turned out to be Howard's tutor? Mr Skin himself—and he was marvellous even if he is enough to give the creeps to Frankenstein's monster. I feel as if I've doubled my chances of a scholarship with just one meeting."

"Well, that's what matters, Genius, isn't it? You've got to learn from him, not fall in love with him! But why are you looking so shifty? Is there something else you've come to tell me?" I bit my lip and nodded.

"He asked me to deliver a message to you. I've got to say that the landlord will collect this month's rent next Saturday—next Saturday, Mog. Even though it was paid last Saturday. Even though I was there myself and saw you hand it over. Howard must be determined to get rid of you this time."

Mog sniffed.

"He was pretty determined last time, but he didn't succeed."

"Aren't you bothered at all then?"

"Not much. I've been expecting something like this. Cheer up, Genius. A lot can happen between now and next Saturday!"

Once again I found myself gaping at our gang leader. Did anything scare her? Was there nothing she couldn't do? Come to that, was there nothing her mum couldn't do judging by what I'd seen a moment ago? Mrs Catley's antics in mid-air would have made Lenny himself wonder if Mog's remarks about her mother mightn't be true after all.

The Death of The Rectifier

A lot could happen before Saturday, that was what Mog said. But what did happen took me completely by surprise. It began with a raid on a graveyard.

"Why there?" I gasped.

Mog grinned a slow Catley-grin.

"Would you think of hiding something there?"

"No."

"Exactly," said Mog. "Neither would anybody else. Especially if our hiding-place is a tomb. Don't look so stunned, Genius. I've checked it all out in advance. There's a grave about the size and shape of a tipped-over wardrobe. It's surrounded by yew trees and on top it's got a loose stone slab. Just perfect."

"In broad daylight?" I asked. "We'll be seen, surely."

"In broad daylight nobody will be looking. Midnight's the time for body-snatchers. Not that we're snatching bodies, of course. More like adding to a body."

This made me even more desperate for an excuse.

"Have we got time, though, Mog? We'd better not be late back to school. You know what Miss Garner's like about lateness."

"Why should we be late? We've both had lunch, we don't have to go out of our way at all and the whole operation should be over in about...oh, ten minutes? So what's the problem? There's acres of time. Probably we'll even get in a game of football before the bell goes. Okay?"

I swallowed.

"Okay."

"You have brought the bag of books, have you?"

"Here. Under my jacket."

"Great. It'll be a cinch, you see. And best of all, His Royal Highness plus Manservant will be up on the heath with their champagne-and-chips picnic. Today we won't be interrupted."

"You seem to have thought of everything."

"Yes I have," she agreed. "Or I've tried to, anyway. We've still got to be prepared for the unexpected though. I'll bet The Rectifier is on his guard every second."

"For what? What could happen?"

Mog shrugged.

"Who knows? We could have slid back the slab, say, and you could be reaching in to see how deep it goes . . . with your fingers brushing cobwebs and mouldering bones . . . and all of a sudden . . . all of a sudden . . ."

I gaped at her, my eyes nearly as wide as my mouth.

". . . . all of a sudden, Genius, a skeleton hand closes over yours . . . *and drags you inside*!"

"Ah!" I shrieked.

"Shall I carry the books?" Mog offered.

I gave them to her so quickly I almost ripped a button from my coat. She was still chuckling when we reached the churchyard.

We slipped in through a side gate. The sky was bright blue and every leaf and every flower looked fresh so the place was probably at its least spooky. For me, though, daytime always looks wrong for gravestones. I prefer the dark for that kind of stillness—preferably with me not there to see it. Ahead of us, the church itself was the colour of cobwebs and mouldering bones. Mog flitted round it keeping to the shadows. I shuffled after her. We reached the yew trees without a glimpse of a vicar or a vampire. Also without a vampire or a vicar glimpsing us. Or so I hoped.

"This is it," Mog whispered.

The tomb was like an open-air altar, much chipped and much stained with bird-lime. Beyond the yew trees we could hear the swish and rumble of traffic.

"Okay, then?" Mog said. "If we both shove hard from this side the whole slab will shift over. Then we'll see if there's enough room to stash our parcel. After that we shift it back and it's our secret for as long as we want."

I stared at the slab. It was as thick as a paving-stone but twice as broad and three times as long. Weather and wildlife had worn away the lettering on its surface. One edge was crumbling. Already there was a gap between the slab and its base. Another three or four inches and we could get the parcel in . . . amongst the cobwebs and mouldering bones. I shuddered again at Mog's words. Surely the worst you'd touch would be a coffin? Unless it had rotted to pieces . . .

"Get a good grip," suggested Mog. "That's it. Now . . . heave!" With my eyes firmly shut I strained at the slab. It shifted not a jot.

"Keep at it," Mog said.

Again I heaved till my muscles ached with effort. Not a fraction of an inch did the slab move.

"Nearly there," Mog commented. "Don't give up, Genius."

Her voice should have come from alongside me. Instead it seemed further away. I opened my eyes and looked round. She was lying on the grass, propped up on her elbows, chewing a leaf.

"Aren't you helping?" I protested.

"I'm having second thoughts," she said. "I think maybe I'll hide the books under that church over there. Think you could shift the steeple over a couple of yards, Genius? Now you've had a bit of practice?"

I gaped at the church and at the tombstone and at her.

"What?" I managed to say.

"You're lovely," Mog spluttered. "You truly are

lovely, Genius. Sometimes I think you believe every-thing I tell you!"

"You mean . . . you mean you're not using the grave as a hiding-place?"

"Of course not, you gorgeous old brainbox you. We'd never shift that slab in a million years. And even if we could, do you really think I'd tamper with someone's grave? Graves are sort of holy. There's a word for spoiling them . . . it's . . . it's . . ."

"Desecration," I said.

"That's it—desecration. The Rectifier would never stoop to that. He's a Man of Honour. You know that, Genius. I couldn't believe it when you started heaving away at a couple of tons of masonry. For a moment I thought you were having *me* on!"

I tried to smile but shifting the slab would have been easier.

"So aren't we here to hide the parcel?" I asked. "If you've finished making a fool of me, that is."

"Don't be upset, Genius. I just couldn't resist pulling your leg. I never thought you'd fall for it. I never thought you'd be so brave either—I'd be terrified of opening up a grave. Yuk! Yet you went right on ahead."

"With desecration," I said bitterly.

"Come on, Genius. You can take a joke, I know. And we've still got the parcel to hide. I found a smashing place over there. It's a kind of hollow stump—"

She broke off. Behind her, sharp as a gunshot, a twig had snapped.

Mog turned slowly. The yew trees fussed gently in the breeze. What was suspicious about that? Just as slowly Mog turned back to me, lifting a finger to her lips. The glint in her eye told me all I needed to know. We backed away, keeping to the open grass this time. My legs felt weighted with tombstones but still I'd have run if Mog had let me. She didn't speak till we were halfway back to school.

"It was him," she said. "Mr Skin."

"Or a cat or a dog," I said. "Or maybe a bird."

"Do you believe that?"

"No. I think it was him, too."

After that we said almost nothing. What Mog was thinking about I've no idea but my own thoughts were in a tangle. Why was Mog being harassed? Was it Howard who was out to get her, or Howard's dad? Even Mog herself had me puzzled. I could understand why she'd set up this project for herself, Rectifier-style, and why she was determined not to be beaten, but was it really worth it? And where did her mum fit in—her droopy, acrobatic mum who was so much like Mog yet so tired all the time? Or nearly all the time, anyway.

The question which baffled me most was what all this had to do with a gawky bookworm on the brink of a scholarship he wanted to win more than anything else in the world. Why should it bother *me*?

At the school gates, Mog paused.

"Here," she said. "Take the parcel, Genius. It's me he'll be after not you. And especially I don't want it at home next Saturday. Keep it in your desk this afternoon and smuggle it home with you. If you want to, that is." I stared at the grubby plastic bag she held out and tried not to let my feelings show. Given the chance I'd have tossed it in the river or in one of the ponds on the heath. At least that would be the end of it. For where would Mog think of hiding it next?

"Are you going to take it, Genius?"

"Okay, Mog," I said.

"You don't look too happy. What's the matter?"

"Nothing.".

"Nothing, my foot! You're not keen, I can see that. Do you want to drop out, Genius? It doesn't matter, you know. It's only a game I'm playing—but all the same I'm determined Howard's not going to win."

"Is he after the parcel then, Mog? Why should he

bother? How does he even know about it?"

"I haven't a clue. He's just out to be a menace, I expect. He doesn't have to menace you, though. It's up to you whether you want to go on with it. Do you?"

"All right. Give it to me. I'll help you hide it. I promise."

"Smashing! I knew you wouldn't let me down, Genius. Now let's play football."

Two minutes later Mog was tackling and passing and shooting just like any other kid—except that she was a lot better than any other kid. As usual, I watched from the sideline. She scored her first with a neat header just inside the coats piled up as a goalpost. Her second came after a fancy piece of footwork round the goalkeeper and her third scorched over the surface of the playground from her own half of the field. The mums who looked after us at lunchtime led the clapping. Mog was a great favourite with them and with everybody else who knew her. Apart from one person, of course.

"Stinky show-off," said that one person.

"Could you do any better?" I demanded, swinging round.

Howard wrinkled his nose.

"With a bit of practice."

"Mog doesn't practise much. Mostly she plays in goal. You're back early, Howard. Where's your tame gorilla?"

"Skin's got a couple of hours off. So my dad brought me back in the Rolls. He's asked me to say something to you by the way."

"Your dad?"

"That's right. He says don't bother to come for any more lessons."

"Why not?"

"Don't you know?"

Howard's face twisted into what my mum calls a grin-and-bear-it expression. It reminded me of the way he'd looked yesterday evening—nasty but also sad.

"No, I don't know," I said.

"He remembered where he'd seen you before."

"Oh . . . the museum."

"Correct."

Was I angry or relieved? I couldn't tell.

"Your dad really must hate The Rectifier," I said.

"Like poison. So do I. When we heard the news at lunchtime we cheered and cheered. I suppose you burst into tears."

I stared at him blankly. Deep in my stomach I felt a cube of ice forming.

"What news at lunchtime?"

"Didn't you hear? It was on the radio. Don't you go home to dinner?"

"Yes but I . . . I was busy. What news are you talking about? Something to do with The Rectifier?"

Howard smirked.

"More like something that's been done to The Rectifier. That Mog of yours will be most interested, I reckon."

A shout of excitement made us turn our heads. Mog had scored goal number four. Almost at once the bell rang for afternoon school. Howard was already hurrying off to be first in the line.

I felt dazed as lessons began. Had something happened to The Rectifier? What had Howard meant? Across the classroom he was bursting with smugness because he knew something the rest of us didn't know. Once, catching my eye, he stuck out his tongue.

His special knowledge didn't last long. After the register Miss Garner handed back some maths work, then came a TV programme. This was always switched on a couple of minutes early to warm up the television set and to warm us up, Miss Garner said. She lowered the sun-blinds and told us to shift our chairs—quietly— so we were all facing the screen.

"And let's do without all the fidgeting with pencils we had last week," she added sharply.

She needn't have worried. We were just in time for a newsflash that froze all pencils in mid-fidget.

The camera was panning over a stretch of river deep in the city—a stretch overlooked by embankments and terraced restaurants and posh office blocks with rooftop gardens. A yacht was moored there. It was white as a swan and elegant enough for a royal family.

"... and it belongs to Hugo Carness, reputed to be the richest man in Europe," said the news reporter. "Only a hundred yards from here the damaged diving-equipment was found along with the waterproof satchel. In it was information that can be linked with the man known as The Rectifier. Was he scouting out Mr Carness as his next victim? Mr Carness was much in the news recently after a dispute with the Inland Revenue. However, the millionaire/financier denies all knowledge of what experts say may have been an underwater mishap in the early hours of this morning. River police are on the look-out for more evidence and, possibly, for a body. Is this The Rectifier's last adventure? For more than two years he has waged a private war against income-tax fraud. All three of the main political parties have condemned his interference in the affairs of the Inland Revenue yet his contributions to the public purse have steadily increased: only this week a major property company has been forced to admit to millions of pounds in unpaid taxes following an investigation by The Rectifier. Now it seems such raids may be over. If so there will be many sighs of regret and just as many sighs of relief. For a full report on this mystery-man whose skill and daring has dazzled both his fans and his critics, watch our main news at five forty-five."

On screen the picture dissolved into a clock and the title music for our school's programme. We watched as if in a trance. The classroom was so quiet you'd have thought it was empty. For most of us it was the world that was suddenly empty. It was like losing your favourite pop star, footballer and comic-strip hero in the same split second.

When the programme finished Miss Garner showed what a good teacher she was. She said nothing at all about the newsflash. She knew we'd come round to it when we were ready. Or maybe she was just as upset as we were because though we had silent reading for the rest of the afternoon nobody remembered to pull up the blinds. In a silent, foot-shuffling dimness split by shafts of sunlight we turned over page after page till school ended.

Outside in the playground the brightness made us blink. It also woke us up. Most of the class mooched around as if reluctant to go home. What was waiting there except the main news at five forty-five?

"I reckon he's had it this time," Lenny said. "I always said he'd cop it eventually."

"Why are you so fed up about it?" asked Alex. "I thought you were against The Rectifier."

Lenny blushed.

"I said me and my dad didn't agree with him. That doesn't mean I'm glad to see him get drowned. If he was drowned. Strikes me that millionaire may have had something to do with it. Probably he got caught . . ."

"And crash-bang-wallop that was that," Alex said.

"Who says he was caught?" said Mog.

We glanced at each other uneasily.

"It stands to reason, Mog," I began. "Even that news reporter seemed to be hinting at it. Once the body's found they'll soon be able to—"

"Who says there's a body?" Mog interrupted.

"Well, there isn't yet but it's obvious that—"

"There's only one thing obvious to me so far. The Rectifier wants everyone to think he's dead. Especially people like the richest man in Europe or whatever Carness is."

"You mean it's a trick?"

"Of course it's a trick, Genius, I'm surprised you haven't seen through it. It's the most dazzling trick of the lot. He lets everybody relax then hits his next victim all the harder—maybe Carness himself!"

Mog eyes sparkled. She was the only kid in our class with a smile on her face.

"I suppose that's possible," I said doubtfully. "We'll just have to wait and see. The newsreels and papers are bound to be full of it for the next few days."

"And all of them more and more certain that The Rectifier is dead," said Mog. "He'll have made sure of that. But I'll bet you one thing . . . no body will ever turn up."

"I wonder . . ." said Alex.

"It would be just like him," Lenny admitted.

"Hey, Mog!" called a voice.

"It's Howard," groaned Alex. "What does he want?"

"Let's see," Mog said.

Followed by most of the kids in the class Howard waddled towards us. Today his windcheater, trousers and shoes were the palest blue. Unlike his face which was the brightest red. He spoke in a shrill, angry voice.

"Hey, Mog. You'll come to my party, won't you?"

"What party, Howard?"

"On Saturday week. It's a Pirate Party. Everybody's got to come dressed as a pirate. My father's booked the *Sark*—we're holding the party on board till midnight."

"The *Sark*?" Lenny exclaimed. "What, the actual sailing ship?"

"That's right. Dad's a director of the Maritime Museum so he's allowed to hire decks and cabins in the *Sark*. We're having pirate games and pirate grub and pirate gold: every kid who comes gets a piece of eight. The party's to celebrate me winning the scholarship."

"But you haven't taken the exam yet," I said. "And the results don't come out till Monday week. That's *after* the party."

Howard sniffed.

"Quite right. But I'm certain to be a winner. Dad says he's got complete confidence in me."

"Who's invited to the party?" asked Mog.

"You are. Your gang is. Everyone in the class is."

"I see."

Suddenly I saw, too. Straight after school Howard had been inviting kid after kid to his party and kid after kid had been saying no. Poor Howard. He'd picked the worst possible moment. If it wasn't Mog upstaging him, it was The Rectifier.

"We'll go to the party if you'll go, Mog!" declared one of the girls.

"Yes!" agreed several others.

"Otherwise Fatty Bygrave can forget it," someone said. "He can stuff his party up his exhaust-pipe."

Everyone laughed except Howard and Mog. Howard was straining to look friendly but he could barely force out the words.

"Will you come to my party, Mog?"

She shrugged.

"On Saturday week? How can I, Howard? I'm not even sure where my mum and I will be living *this* Saturday, let alone the Saturday after. We're having trouble with our landlord, you know. Mind you . . . if we get that sorted out—properly sorted out—I'd love to come."

Howard's face had been red before. Now it was crimson.

"I reckon . . . I reckon you'll get your landlord problems sorted out," he said.

"Do you really think so, Howard? For sure? Absolutely for certain?"

"Yes . . . yes. For sure."

"Okay, folks!" Mog called. "See you at the party!"

A cheer echoed round the playground. You'd have thought it was her party not Howard's. She was surrounded by girls telling her what pirate-dresses they intended to wear and by boys describing the pirate-weapons they were going to make.

"Look at that!" said Lenny in disgust. "They've forgotten about The Rectifier already."

"No they haven't," I said. "They're just concentrating on something else as a relief. To help take their minds off it. It's a well-known psychological mechanism."

"Is that so? I knew you'd have a word for it, Brains."

Lenny went on to say something else but I wasn't listening. I was watching Howard display another well-known psychological mechanism: running away. Head down, he was retreating towards the school gate as fast as his fatness would allow.

Waiting for him there was Mr Skin.

I shivered and clutched Mog's parcel even tighter under my coat. Perhaps she was right and the dawn accident up-river had been a fake. Or perhaps the time had come already for a twelve-year-old girl to take over from The Rectifier.

Scholarship

A week went by—Tuesday to Tuesday—at a speed so slow it was like waiting for Christmas. Sleeping and schoolwork filled most of my time but three things filled most of my thoughts: the scholarship, The Rectifier and the parcel.

Why the parcel?

Even now I can't answer that question. Goodness knows my exam preparation kept me busy. Between dawn and darkness every hour felt like a last-minute rush to get ready. Only news headlines distracted my attention—headlines that said goodbye to The Rectifier over and over again. Yet still there was no body.

And each morning before breakfast and each night before bed I lifted the floorboard to check up on the parcel. I weighed it in my hands. I turned it this way and that. I held it up to the light. All I didn't do was open it.

But bulletins and books in a plastic bag were really just sidelines in my seven-day countdown to the scholarship.

"Relax," said Miss Garner. "You've done everything you can."

"You're winding yourself up much too hard," said Dad. "Be careful you don't jam like a watch and stop ticking."

"Can't you forget it for five minutes?" said Lenny or Alex or both. Mog said nothing, just grinned to wish me well. She never mentioned our unfinished business.

At last, one hundred and seventy hours or so later, the examination arrived.

It began with the meeting of all ten candidates in the school's famous forecourt. We eyed each other carefully. We knew only one full scholarship would be awarded, together with two half-scholarships. That meant there would be one winner, two half-winners and seven losers. Except in my case. For me there would be only one winner and nine losers because a half-scholarship wasn't good enough—Mum and Dad could never raise the money for the other half.

"Fancy your chances?" asked a lanky kid with spectacles.

"Not much," I said.

"What was your grading for the prelim?"

This was a test we'd already taken at our own schools to decide the best kids for today. Miss Garner told me I'd got the highest grade she could ever remember. It was after this people started calling me 'Brains' and 'Genius' and 'Scholarship Boy'.

"I got alpha-minus," I said.

He nodded.

"So did I."

I shrugged as if to suggest we must both have been a bit off-form. Really, I was staggered. How many other kids had done the same? Or even better? I'd expected to be the top scorer.

"Have you been car spotting?" my rival went on. "I've noticed two Jaguars, two Rovers, a BMW, a Bentley and a Ford Granada. I bet I'm the only one who's turned up in a mini—and a battered mini at that."

"I turned up on a bus," I said.

"Did you? Great! One in the eye for the snobs! Car off the road, is it?"

"We haven't got a car."

"Oh?"

"Can't afford it," I said.

"Ah . . . I see."

He meant to laugh as if it didn't matter but he couldn't

get his voice right. Behind his spectacles his eyes blinked and looked anywhere but at me. Perhaps he was afraid I wasn't wearing a shirt or had shoes made of cardboard. He needn't have worried. All my clothes were good and all of them were new. Mum had bought them specially. She'd been saving for months.

"How many motor bikes have you spotted?" I asked.

"Motor bikes?"

"Here comes one now."

"Cripes! Who's he? Friend of yours?"

"Not exactly."

Along with everyone else we watched Howard make his favourite entrance. The Honda swung in a complete circle, its bodywork gleaming black and silver. Even the thudder-thudder-thudder-thudder of the engine sounded highly polished. Mr Skin dismounted first, then Howard. The ritual removal of helmet and leather followed with the chauffeur snapping to attention now and then to make sure we all knew who was boss. Finally he saluted. Howard dismissed him with a jerk of the head.

"Glad to see he's carrying his own pencil-case," grinned the boy in spectacles. "I was beginning to think that sinister-looking slave of his was going to take the exam for him. Does the Black Ogre accompany him everywhere?"

"Pretty nearly. Where Howard Bygrave is, Mr Skin's not far behind."

"Good reason for steering clear of Howard Bygrave, if you ask me."

"That's what we all say. It's harder than you think."

It was harder even than I thought. All that morning Mr Skin seemed to be peering over my shoulder. He'd predicted detail after detail of what we had to do: about the tour of the school, for example, led by a senior master in a flowing gown. We walked in cloisters that reminded me of monks poring over manuscripts and through quadrangles where the grass was so smooth I imagined a dozen barbers shaving it daily with cut-throat razors. All this Mr Skin had described exactly—like the low, rug-strewn dormitories where the boarders slept. Also he was right about the dining-hall, a vault of ancient oak-panelling hung with portraits that seemed to have grown in the frame. His most vivid prophecy, though, concerned the library where we were to sit the written part of the exam. When I saw the long walls of red-and-gold-bound books I recognised them instantly. Would his acount of the exam itself be as accurate?

At first glance I saw that here too he'd briefed us thoroughly. The layout of the questions, the print and even the feel of the paper between finger and thumb was just what he'd told us to expect. Was I really seeing these maths problems for the first time? Hadn't I come across this poem before? It was uncanny. In just one lesson he'd made it all so familiar to me I almost felt I was cheating. But before I could gloat over my good luck I noticed that everyone else was writing just as quickly and intently as I was. Especially Howard. And how many lessons with Mr Skin had *he* had? Enough to do better than me? My mouth went dry at the thought. I finished writing in a frenzy. Yet still I forced myself to take Mr Skin's advice and spend the last ten minutes of the exam reading through what I'd written, word by word.

"How do you think you did?" asked the tall boy with the glasses.

I shrugged.

"Okay, I suppose."

"A fair paper, I reckon," he said.

"Reasonable," I agreed.

Really, thanks to Mr Skin, the paper had seemed easy to me. From my check-through I was sure I'd made no silly mistakes. Also I'd managed plenty of clevernesses of the kind that made Miss Garner purr like a cat full of goldfish.

"A pleasure to mark," I could hear her say.

"Mind you, there's still the interview to come," continued His Lankiness. "That's the bit that scares me. I still haven't made up my mind which approach to adopt. I mean, do you just speak your mind or do you tell them what you think they want to hear? The first way you risk getting up their noses with opinions they don't like, the second way you could end up sounding like a horrible little crawler. Which do you reckon?"

"No idea."

This was true. During our lesson Mr Skin hadn't mentioned the interview. Could he have saved this for when Howard was on his own?

"What's the matter? You've gone green all of a sudden."

"Nothing," I said quickly.

"You sure?"

"Of course I'm sure."

"It's probably the effect of being cooped up all morning," he said. "On a day like this it's enough to make anyone green. Feel a bit queasy myself as a matter of fact. Sometimes I wonder if it's worth it."

I glanced round the classroom where we'd been having lunch. It was a bare-walled, dull room full of the first desks ever invented. The stone-carved windows also had a bygone look. Yet through them I could see future professors and brain surgeons and prime-ministers tipping their straw hats to each other in the sunshine ... my personal Popocatapetl that's what the scholarship meant to me.

"It's worth it all right," I said.

Across the room sat Howard, his gaze far, far away. Perhaps he was on his Honda, zooming towards some dream horizon. Or perhaps he was recalling Mr Skin's lessons about the interview. Speak your mind? Or tell them what you think they want to hear? I knew which I preferred but which would win the scholarship? If Mog hadn't annoyed Howard's dad so much in the museum I might have found out. Probably one more session with

Mr Skin would have been enough. Why, oh why, hadn't I stayed at home that Saturday morning?

"Hello," muttered Goggles. "We've started. And I bet I'm first." The door had opened and an old man in a white jacket came in . He was a school servant called an usher.

"Peter Annersley," he called. "The Headmaster is ready."

"Told you it would be me."

"Good luck," I said.

"Ta."

Nine pairs of eyes watched him as he left. Soon it would be the turn of the next person, and the next, and the next . . .

And finally it was my name being announced. The usher led me along a gallery lined with photographs behind glass—cricket and rugby teams, athletes caught in mid-stride, swimmers, tennis players and some boys on horseback. Would I have to join in all those? Where would I get the kit, especially a horse? There seemed to be pictures of every sport in existence except big game hunting. And soccer. Maybe after all I should settle for football and the Comprehensive . . . like the gibbering, tearful scaredycat that all of a sudden I was.

"Good luck, son," said the usher as he showed me into the Headmaster's study.

I nodded miserably.

The long, grey room came as a surprise. It felt like entering a drawer in a giant filing cabinet. Where had all the history gone? At the far end were three men in bank-manager suits.

"Come and take a chair," one said.

Chair? What chair? I stared round me in a panic. Was it some kind of trick?

"Over here."

He pointed. There? Right in the middle of them? With lowered eyes I crossed the room and sat down.

"Thank you for coming," said the same, friendly voice. "It's no fun scribble-scribble-scribbling on a warm day and then having to chat to perfect strangers. I'm the Headmaster, by the way."

"Are you?" I said in surprise.

"Oh dear! I seem to have disappointed you already. What were you expecting?"

"Well I . . . I expected you to be wearing one of those robe-things."

"And a mortar-board?" he laughed. "With a cane under my arm? There are moments when I wear a cap and gown, yes. But not when I'm meeting a youngster for the first time and want to put him at his ease. This, by the way, is the school chaplain, Mr Mayfield."

"Hello," said Mr Mayfield.

He was a tiny gnome of a man in a vicar's collar who looked like somebody's great-great-great-grandfather. The Headmaster looked like everybody's favourite uncle. I almost sighed with relief.

"And this is the Chairman of our governors," the Headmaster continued, "Sir Edwin Fitzlyon."

"Good afternoon," said Sir Edwin.

I tried to reply but my mouth wouldn't work. Once again I was struck by the Curator's thin-ness and his hands—like a skeleton wearing baseball gloves. Also I was hypnotised by the sharpness of his look. Was it recognition I saw there?

"I believe this young fellow and I have met once already, Headmaster. At the museum."

"Oh? A school party?"

"No. This was more of a private party."

"Are you interested in the sea?" asked Mr Mayfield.

"A bit," I said.

They waited for me to go on. But what more was there to say? I felt I might as well pack up and return home there and then. Lenny would have left. So would Alex, probably.

And Mog?

I didn't want to think about Mog.

"What *is* your greatest interest, then?" asked the Headmaster. "Apart from winning a scholarship, that is. Every candidate feels he's got to put that first. What else really fascinates you?"

I gritted my teeth. What did it matter now?

"The Rectifier," I said.

The three men seemed to wake up.

"You're the first lad this afternoon to say that," the Chaplain said.

"Really? I suppose they don't think it's posh enough. Probably they think you'd prefer glass-blowing or building their own radio sets."

"But you think that—secretly—they're just as fascinated by The Rectifier as you?"

"They must be. Just about everyone I know is."

"Why is that do you think?"

I shrugged. Why should I bother with all this chit-chat now? Still, Mum and Dad had told me I must never be rude so I'd better continue—even though I knew already Mog had destroyed my chances of a scholarship two Saturdays and two centuries ago.

"I suppose The Rectifier is fascinating because he's an outlaw . . . but an outlaw who's on the side of what's right. Like Robin Hood. But *he's* got more against him than the Sheriff of Nottingham and bad King John. *Everybody's* against him in a way because today you're not allowed to take the law into your own hands. There's no place in our society for vigilantes. So he's on his own. He hasn't even got Richard the Lionheart to back him up. Nobody's going to come home from the Crusades to give The Rectifier a free pardon. He's the loneliest man in England."

"If he is a man," said Sir Edwin drily. "Any reason why The Rectifier couldn't be . . . female?"

"No reason at all. He could be anybody. He could be one of us sitting here now."

The Chaplain shifted in his chair and fingered his dog-collar.

"I hardly think that's likely," he sniffed.

"People like The Rectifier aren't ever likely," I said. "He's an anachronism—someone who belongs to a different age."

"How true. You must have found his death very sad."

I frowned.

"If he is dead."

"Doesn't all the evidence suggest he is?"

"All the evidence except a body does. But suppose he's planted the evidence? Suppose that's what he wants everybody to think?"

"To take the heat off?" said the Headmaster. "That's possible."

"The Rectifier makes anything possible," I went on. "It's the most marvellous thing about him. He makes adventure something that can happen anywhere, anyday. He can turn ordinary life into a sort of Golden Land, full of Golden Dreams . . . like in that poem by WJ Turner."

"*Romance*?" asked Sir Edwin.

"That's the one."

"Tell us about it."

So I did—how-many-beans-make-five and all. They listened very politely. But it was nothing more than politeness because soon afterwards the interview was over. There were none of the questions Miss Garner had told me to expect about which languages I wanted to learn or what sports I wanted to play or whether I'd decided on a career.

"Alas, we haven't any more time," the Headmaster said.

Any more time to *waste* was what he meant. I followed the usher out of the room and down the corridor without a word. Every footstep sounded like Mog-Mog-Mog-Mog-Mog-Mog-Mog-Mog. Why hadn't I stayed at home that Saturday morning?

At the school gates, Dad was waiting.

"I've brought the limousine to meet you," he joked.

Behind him was a gleaming red Post Office van.

"How did you get on?"

"The written paper was okay but I've failed on the interview."

"Did they tell you that?"

"I just know."

"And when do you find out if the school agrees with you?"

"They'll agree with me all right. We get a letter next Monday. Or maybe a telegram before that if we've won anything. But there won't be any telegram for me, Dad. I'm certain."

"Well, I daresay you did your best, son. That's the important thing." From the gruffness of his voice I could tell he was disappointed. I slid back the door of the van and clambered in. Before I could close it again Peter Annersley had seen me.

"Hey—that's a bit better than a bus," he called. "It's a bit better than a battered mini, too. Cheerio! Hope you did well in the exam."

"You too," I said. "Cheers."

"Who was that?" Dad asked.

"Oh, some kid."

Some kid who I'll never see again I wanted to add.

Our route home was a trip through Mog-country. We passed the bridge where she'd tried to rescue the bird and the church where she'd had me heave-hoing several hundred-weight of tomb. Crossing the heath, I saw marks on the grass where she'd provoked Howard into his one-bike stampede. Also I caught a glimpse of our playground—scene of the great hand-walking contest. For a couple of hundred yards we even drove alongside the Quaggy. I couldn't get away from Mog.

"Look over there!" Dad exclaimed with a fake cheerfulness. High above us soared masts and spars, linked by a network of stay and halliard.

"The *Sark*, son. Finest sailing ship ever! Not long now to the party . . ." Mog's party, I thought.

"And there's the museum . . . the best maritime collection in the world!"

When we pulled up outside our house I was close to tears. Mum was peeking through the front room curtains but she was on the doorstep before Dad had even switched off the engine.

"How did you—"

From the corner of my eye I saw Dad shaking his head at her.

"I'll be up in my room, Mum," I said huskily. "Call me when supper's ready."

For an hour I lay on my bed. Downstairs I heard Mum and Dad creeping about as if not to disturb an invalid. Every tick-tock of my alarm clock repeated the same question . . . why-why, why-why, why-why, why-why hadn't I stayed at home that Saturday morning? It was a silly question because I knew the answer already: Mog. Did I have any real choice when Mog was around? She had only to throw a stone at my window even now and I'd follow her on another parcel-hiding expedition. Wouldn't I? Or would I . . .? I rolled over and reached down to the loose floorboard. To stop this nonsense all I needed to do was get rid of the parcel.

"Sorry," I'd say. "Some kids snatched it from me and chucked it in the river. Sank like a stone. Doesn't matter much, does it?"

I slotted the floorboard back into place and hoisted the plastic bag on to the bed. It mattered to Mog. I'd seen the look in her eyes. In a way the parcel was *her* scholarship. So why shouldn't she fail it, like me?

Tug by tug I loosened the knot. My first astonishment was the cleanness of the books once they were outside their covering. The pages of handwriting and columns of figures were neat and fresh enough to have come straight from any business office. My second astonishment was finding the name *Catley* towards the back of the book. Under the title *Rent* there was a list of payments.

Then came the biggest astonishment of all. It crept up on me slowly till I felt ambushed by shock. Quickly I leafed through each volume again not believing the evidence. Yet I knew it was true. These were the secret accounts of Howard Bygrave Senior. Every one of his shady deals was recorded here, adding up to the price of a Carness-type yacht. How had Mog got hold of them? They'd have been a prize for The Rectifier himself. Unless Mog really was ... no, that was impossible. Certainly she was as tough as a stunt-man and as limber as a high-wire artist but where would a twelve-year-old girl get the know-how? For that she'd need to be much older, at least as old as . . . as her mother.

"Supper's ready!" called Dad.

I scarcely heard him. I was deafened by the sound of questions and answers slotting into place. Now I knew why Mog was so convinced The Rectifier was alive. She *lived* with The Rectifier. By day her mum pretended to be a limp, lazy lady without visible means of support. By night she hunted treasure. From the start this had been no dummy-run like Mog's trial in the museum; it had been a *real* test with real risks and a real prize at stake. Mog wasn't pretending. She *was* apprentice to The Rectifier. No wonder Mr Skin's suspicions had been aroused. Perhaps my own suspicions would have been aroused too if I hadn't been distracted by the scholarship.

"Any reason why The Rectifier couldn't be... female?" Sir Edwin had asked. No reason at all. I'd stumbled on the best kept secret in the land.

And right now I couldn't have cared less.

Sark

Saturday arrived like a party present for Howard. By breakfast-time the sky was already so blue you knew it would last till nightfall. Till the last possible moment, that is, for him or for me to get a telegram from the school. All day I waited for a miracle.

"Maybe your father will bring it home from the sorting-office," said my mum. "He's on late-turn tonight."

I pulled a couldn't-care-less face.

"And you'd better get your costume on, my lad, or you'll be late."

"No I won't, Mum. Alex and his dad are picking me up in their car. They'll be bringing me home again, too."

"Thanks for letting us know."

"Sorry, I forgot . . . I . . . I've had a lot on my mind."

"I know you have, son."

Mum turned her head away quickly but not before I'd caught the look in her eyes. She also had been waiting all day.

Most of the kids I knew had been waiting all day. But for them relief came at eight o'clock on the waterfront.

"It's . . . it's like the Spanish Main," someone said.

"Like Tortuga," said another. "You know, that city for pirates."

So it was in a way. The Bygraves couldn't get rid of the housing estate alongside the *Sark*, or of the cranes and chimneys that fringed the river. What they had managed to do was hang lanterns above the surrounding pavements to match the ship's decks and galleys and cabins and holds. These were lit already as if for an early dusk. Or an early weighing of anchor: despite the concrete in which it was docked and its spars empty of sail, the *Sark* looked ready to cast off. There was just breeze enough to thrum in its rigging. Its flags and pennants seemed to be flapping goodbye. Actually, they signalled the word 'Greetings'. This, and every other detail of what we had to look forward to, Howard had told us in advance.

"I'm surprised he hasn't issued a programme," Lenny said.

"Or a script," said Mog. "Do you get the feeling, now and again, you're being set up? That all this is a kind of trap?"

"What do you mean?"

"Oh . . . just a feeling."

We laughed nervously and fingered our invitations. These had a skull-and-cross-bones emblem and were printed in smudgy, blood-red lettering.

"But whose blood?" Alex asked. "Not Howard's, I bet."

"Howard's blood would be blue," I said. "According to him he's descended from kings and princes."

"Get off!" said Lenny. "Howard's blood would be green—the colour of folding-money."

Alex giggled.

"Has Howard got any blood at all? He's not exactly a normal human being, is he? My guess is that deep in all that fat he's kept going by a clockwork motor. I bet Mr Skin's first job every day is to wind Howard up! Now where would he keep the key, I wonder . . ."

"When's he going to let us on board?" Lenny interrupted. "That's what I want to know."

Several kids were asking this. We'd been queuing at the foot of the gang-plank for twenty minutes now. Already we knew who was dressed as what and had each come to the conclusion our own costume was the best of the lot. There were tavern wenches, stowaways and

cabin-boys, three Nelsons and a couple of Francis Drakes, as well as a host of Blackbeards and Long John Silvers. Alex, though, was definitely the best Sinbad and Lenny the best Viking. And I was the only Ben Gunn.

It was the way Mog was dressed which surprised us. She wore a loose, frilled shirt and tight breeches with her legs bare below the knee. Hers was the only *dirty* costume. No fancy-dress for Mog. She looked like the real thing.

"A real what, though?" asked a girl.

"I'm a powder-monkey," Mog said. "I carry the gunpowder from the locker down below to the cannons on the gun-decks. Without me there'd be no broadsides or explosions."

"You can say that again!" agreed Lenny.

"Hey!" came a voice. "They've opened the doors. It's Howard!"

He stood at the top of the gang-plank. No one spoke as we all stared up at him. His crown and his robe and his trident gleamed like fish-scales. The breeze lifted his seaweed hair and his seaweed beard. Even his sandals looked made from seaweed.

"King Neptune welcomes you!" he announced shrilly.

Behind us there was a flurry of laughter.

"What did they say?" I asked.

"Howard-and-chips," Lenny repeated.

"Shush," said Mog. "Be polite. It is Howard's party."

Howard wasn't going to let us forget it. Every guest was a kid he saw daily at school yet he still scrutinised each invitation as though it might have been a forgery presented by a total stranger. When he got to me he frowned.

"What's that?" he demanded, pointing at my chest.

I glanced down. From my shaggy tunic stuck a corner of Mog's plastic-bag. My breathing and my heartbeat almost stopped dead.

"Have you brought your own sandwiches?" Howard said.

His joke saved me. By the time he'd finished laughing at it Howard had lost interest in the package. Unlike Mr Skin. The chauffeur stood as straight and as still as he always did, not moving a muscle. Except his eyes.

"Why is the Bygrave Bogyman looking at you like that, Genius?" asked Alex. I swallowed.

"Don't know."

"I'd steer clear of him if I were you."

"Thanks for the advice," I said bitterly.

How do you steer clear of somebody when you're both on the same ship? Eventually we were bound to meet face to face—perhaps in some corner of the vessel where we'd be alone. I could see it happening . . . a huge figure in black leathers and corduroy towering over a spindly, shivering bookworm dressed in animal furs. I shuddered. Somehow I had to be rid of the parcel. But where? Wasn't it up to Mog to decide on a hiding-place? She was supposed to be the powder-monkey yet it was me hugging the explosive. For Mr Skin had guessed what we'd brought to the party, I was convinced of that. Sooner or later he'd make his move.

"Have you been down below?" someone said. "It's incredible—the main hold is all set up like a treasure-cave. There's a disco, too, with lights, amplifiers, the lot! Howard's dad must've spent a fortune."

"Wait till you get to the galley," came the answer. "I've never seen such food! It makes Christmas dinner look like a packed lunch! And there's a barbecue with two chefs to cook anything you want right there on the spot."

"The grog's not bad either," declared a third voice. "Not exactly pirate-rum but pretty potent stuff. Howard says it's been brewed to a special recipe. There's barrels of it. You just grab a tankard and help yourself." Before long we'd heard about the continuous film-show in the fo'c's'le and the shooting-gallery aft where you could learn to fire a pirate-pistol or musket. Also word reached us of the area amidships with its masks and gloves and padded jackets for cutlass-fighting—with every size and shape of cutlass provided. Nobody mentioned the quoits and hoopla you could play up on deck. After all, as Howard was the first to point out, *every* luxury-liner has those.

"So where's the blinkin' swimming-pool?" said Lenny.

Howard shrugged like a sea-majesty.

"Didn't you notice it? Up at the bowsprit end of the ship? After dark it'll be floodlit."

"And freezing," objected a girl. "Not to mention the fact that you didn't warn us to bring swimsuits. What are we supposed to do, Howard, bathe in the nude?"

"If you like," said Howard. "But that's not what I've planned." With a fat-lipped grin on his face he turned away. Mr Skin followed him below.

Next came two astonishing hours, an interval it's impossible for me to explain. Maybe from terror or a brainstorm I forgot everything—yes, the parcel, The Rectifier and the scholarship. I even forgot Mr Skin. I felt like a little kid at a fairground for the first time.

"Brains is enjoying himself," I heard Alex say.

"About time," Lenny said. "He worries too much."

"Not now he isn't," laughed Alex.

Even Mog couldn't keep up with me. I fenced and fired, watched a film, ate, drank, danced, hoopla'd and threw quoits as if the party were some kind of pentathlon and I had to score a record number of points. Twice Mog tried to draw me aside.

"Later, Mog," I said. "There's plenty of time to find a hiding-place."

"Is there? I thought you'd want to get it over with, Genius. I've got a plan for a decoy—"

"Later," I insisted.

After her second attempt, much puzzled, Mog gave up.

Darkness took over the vessel, shadow by shadow. Except at the bowsprit end of the ship. Here in a blaze of light was Neptune's water-garden. The pool was about two metres deep and six metres in diameter with a platform all round it to help us see better. See what? Well, Neptune himself for a start. Howard stood with his trident poised as though to quell a tidal wave. Why had he sent Mr Skin to gather us there? Eager to know, we fell quiet. Or most of us did. Two girls went on chattering.

"Silence!" piped Howard.

Before they could reply a figure moved in the darkness behind them. Both girls stiffened and clamped their mouths shut. Mr Skin had whispered something. Slowly Howard lowered the trident. His shrill voice was raised in the half-chant he always used when he was trying to be dramatic.

"Seafarers! The time has come for The Jonah Game."

He paused as well he might. What was he talking about? All round the pool kids shrugged and shook their heads at each other.

"The Jonah Game," Howard went on, "is a contest from long, long ago. It was played by pirates in Tortuga Bay. In those days a plank of wood was stretched over the sea between two ships . . . like this."

Mr Skin laid a plank from one edge of the pool to the other and fixed it in place. It was about as wide as your foot turned sideways.

"On this plank," continued Howard, "a member of each ship's crew would balance, both men blindfolded but facing each other. They were given a map or navigation-chart tightly bound till it was the shape and length of a fat cutlass . . . like these." Mr Skin held up two folded parchments.

"Then the two men tried to clout each other as hard as they could. This way." With both parchments in one hand, Mr Skin slapped the plank. The crack-crack as contact was made echoed off the *Sark*'s flat surfaces.

"Of course, since they couldn't see each other there were more misses than hits. To win the game you had to knock your opponent off the plank into the water—or get him to fall in by overbalancing from one of his own clouts. The loser was reckoned to be a Jonah, someone who brings bad luck to a ship. He had to swim ashore and make certain he was never seen again."

"I've never heard of this game," Lenny whispered. "Have you come across it, Brains?"

"Not in any of the books I've read."

"Do you suppose Howard's invented it?" Alex asked.

Before we could reply, Howard had issued another invitation.

"Now who'd like to play The Jonah Game with me? Anyone dare?"

"With you, Howard?" someone said.

"With me. Just to show I'm not frightened of being Jonah myself. Remember that the loser not only gets a ducking, he's got to leave the ship, too. No more party for him. That's if we play the game properly."

"Wait a minute, Howard. Does that mean if *you* end up in the drink *you've* got to leave the party? And you'll still let the rest of us carry on without you?"

"Of course. Fair's fair."

This brought a hubbub of talk. Most of us were in agreement that Howard's party was spoiled only by one thing—the presence of Howard himself, plus Mr Skin. Was this a chance to get rid of them both?

"So who's going to fight me?" asked Howard.

He must have known who we'd choose. Only one person would risk being expelled early from the best Saturday night we'd ever had—like Cinderella having to leave the ball at ten instead of twelve. Yet Mog still seemed surprised when we turned to her.

"Doesn't someone else want the chance?"

She was truly astonished that no one did.

"Okay, then . . . if you're sure I'm not doing someone

else out of it." Our cheer rang round the *Sark* as if we were sea-weary mariners who'd spotted land for the first time in months.

"I hope you've got your water-proof knickers on, Howard," shouted Lenny.

"Let's hope Mog has," Howard snapped. "Oh . . . there's one rule I forgot. Don't look so worried all of you. It applies to both of us. The pirates in the olden days were very strict about it. The Jonah Game had to be played *in complete silence*. Not a word from anyone, whatever happened. If a person spoke while it was going on his tongue was torn out immediately. We won't do that, of course, but do you all agree to watch without making a sound? Whatever happens? Do you?"

"Is that all right with you, Mog?" Alex asked.

"Fine," agreed Mog. "It's so each fighter can hear every move the other one makes, I suppose. Okay, kids? Not a word during the game . . . whatever happens." We nodded, still doubtful. Since when had Howard been so brave?

"Strict quiet," repeated Howard. "You all agree to that? Cross your hearts and hope to die?"

Uneasily, we nodded again.

"Do it, then," he demanded.

In the darkness beyond the floodlights more than thirty kids lifted their right hands, made a cross over their hearts and scraped a finger over their throats.

"Cross our hearts and hope to die," we all muttered.

Thus Howard got his vow of silence, though why he wanted it nobody knew. Not a word would be uttered now even if a shark's fin appeared above the surface of the pool or even if Mog were dive-bombed suddenly by a squadron of Bygrave-trained, Kamikaze seagulls.

It was so quiet as Mog and Howard took up their positions on the strip of wood you could hear the flutter of the pennants high up in the darkness and the creak of the lanterns on their fixings. All that was missing was the crash of the sea and the sound of timber and canvas at full stretch. I felt like an extra on a dumb-struck film set with every eye on the villain and the hero.

Even with the scarf round her face Mog made the plank look as wide as a paving-stone. She took quick, flat paces with feet spread in the style of a tightrope-walker. Halfway across she paused and listened for Howard. He hadn't taken a step, yet. With his glittering, salmon-coloured robes and wig made of seaweed he looked at his bulkiest and most awkward. Mog had to be an easy winner.

Then Howard solved the mystery. He lifted a finger to his lips, crossed his heart and scraped his throat. We fidgeted in annoyance at the reminder to keep quiet. Who needed it?

We did. A second later. It was a cheat so simple Howard revealed it in a moment. *He took off his blindfold.*

We gnashed our teeth, shook our fists, clawed and strangled with our hands, karate-chopped thin air and mimed hate at Howard in every possible way. He took no notice at all. Poor Mog. Everyone could see what was coming except her.

His face twisted with spite, Howard edged towards Mog. Could she hear him approach? She prodded in front of her to gauge his distance. Howard giggled and lashed her across the face. Smack! In mid-stagger, Mog was already hitting back. Her parchment-weapon thwacked against his leg so hard he yelped with dismay. Had he lost his balance? Not quite. The plank trembled into stillness as they both recovered.

What Howard had lost was some of his cockiness. His second attack was much more wary. He advanced in a tiptoe-crouch. Her ankles were his target this time—one step sideways from the shock of his blow and he knew she'd topple. Inch by inch he got in position. He drew back his weapon. Twice Mog swept the air just over his head. We held our breath as Howard struck . . . too late.

By guesswork or some sixth sense she was ahead of him. She skipped over his cutless and brought her own swooping down across Howard's head and shoulders. His screech was more from fury than pain but it was all Mog needed. Thrash-thrash-thrash across his shoulders came two forehands and a backhand—enough to give her set and match on a tennis-court. Also enough to give her The Jonah Game.

"Aaaaaaaagh!"

Reeling away from her, Howard slipped. In a slow motion panic of arms and legs he belly-flopped into the water. The splash was like a slow bomb-burst.

"Hurray!"

Our cheer must have been heard across the heath. Before it had died away Mog's blindfold was off and she was reaching a hand to Howard. He wanted no help from her. Cursing, spitting water, he floundered to the side of the pool.

"Cheerio, Neptune!" came a voice.

"Now it's soggy Howard-and-chips," exclaimed Alex.

"Can we talk now, Howard?" Lenny asked. "Or would you prefer us to go on laughing?"

"Look out, folks!" the first voice continued, "I can see the Loch Ness Bygrave!"

"Aaa—choo!" Howard sneezed.

"Bless you!" shouted every kid on the *Sark*.

Or almost every kid. One exception was Mog. It wouldn't be fair to describe her expression as goody-goody. She just looked sad. But what about? Could she really be feeling sorry for her enemy?

"Hey, Mog!" Lenny yelled. "Cheer up! You're the champ!"

This started everyone off.

"Catley—the King of Clobber!"

"Cosher-Catley!"

"Mog the Masher!"

"Catley-the-Clout!"

And so on. Through it all, Mog said nothing. Not even when she was told about Howard's cheating. Her eyes never left him as he was wrapped in blankets by Mr Skin.

"Howard!" she called suddenly.

One word from her was enough to quieten us all.

"Howard!"

"What?"

"Will you do me a favour—a great favour?"

"Why should I?"

"If you do I'll let you stay on the ship. You needn't go ashore." Slowly Howard turned to face her.

"Not go ashore? How come? What's the favour?"

"It will be a bit dangerous," Mog said.

"Dangerous?"

"Yes, Howard. Will you let me try it? In return for ditching that stupid rule about you missing the rest of the party? It's something I've always wanted to do ever since I first saw the *Sark*."

"Huh?" said Howard, suspiciously. "What's that?"

Mog's head tilted. At first we thought she was looking up at the stars. They were framed in a tangle of rigging that criss-crossed high above us like a safety-net to stop night from crashing down on the vessel. It was this rigging that held her gaze.

"Go up there," said Mog. "That's what I want to do. Climb up there to the crow's nest, to the highest point you can reach on the *Sark*. Just for the fun of it. Okay?"

"You want to climb up there? In the dark?"

"Dark or daylight what does it matter? Whichever it was the sailors had to go up aloft when they were at sea. Imagine what it must've been like with the ship pitching and tossing in a high wind . . ."

"Suppose you fall?"

"I'll make sure I fall in the swimming-pool."

Mog laughed and stood on tiptoe lifting her arms like a high-diver. Suddenly I noticed two buttons of her shirt had come undone at the waist. I also noticed a plastic-bag tucked into the top of her belt. Till now her frills and flounces had hidden it. With both hands I grabbed at my own stomach. The books, in their wrapping, were still hidden beneath my furs. So what was Mog doing with this second package?

"Go ahead then," Howard agreed. "No one will stop you. Providing . . ."

"Yes?"

". . . providing I'm released from being Jonah."

"Fine. That's what I said. You can stay on the ship."

Mog lowered her arms slowly and turned round in a complete circle. Wherever he was Mr Skin must have glimpsed her parcel. It was as if she wanted him to see it.

And all at once I understood. She *did* want him to see it. This package was the decoy. Her plan was to fool Mr Skin into thinking the Bygrave account-books were hidden aloft amongst the stays and halliards of the *Sark*. It would be a day, maybe two days, before he discovered the truth. By then she'd have found another secret place. Or maybe her mum would have finished off this episode in Mog's training by sending the books to the Government.

"She's daft," said Lenny. "Stark staring bonkers."

If only he knew. I hugged the real parcel tight as Mog began to climb.

"Switch off the lights," someone suggested. "So we can see her."

"So we can see her *fall*," Lenny added.

Howard clicked his fingers and the floodlights doused.

"She's hooked a lantern to her belt," said Alex. "That'll make it easier."

"You reckon?" Lenny said. "She's mad I tell you. The risk isn't worth it. It's like rescuing that bird on the railway bridge all over again. Except there isn't a bird this time. Not even a dead one."

"Oh, Mog'll be all right. Think of her hand-walking

and somersaults and stuff. And you've seen how good she is on the wall-bars at school."

"Alex," said Lenny. "The wall-bars at school don't sway about. And you don't climb them by moonlight."

"I suppose not," Alex admitted.

"Just watch," I said.

"Shouldn't we move amidships?" asked the kid standing next to me. "That's where she's going up."

"Won't be such a good view as she gets higher," his neighbour pointed out.

"Also she might land on top of you if she falls," said Lenny.

From the darkness of the deck we stared up at the darkness of the sky. Night had thickened around the *Sark's* masts and spars and the mesh of cable they supported. Without canvas, what had all this to do with a sailing ship? It was more like an electric web of pylon and aerial—with only the glow from the lantern to tell us that spider Mog was moving higher and higher.

"She'll never make it," said Alex. "Not up and down again."

"Yes she will," I said.

Rung by rung, rope by rope, Mog climbed. No ladder was as steep or as tall as this.

"She's actually going faster," Lenny said. "Just look! She's almost there."

"Don't rush, Mog," I begged.

By now the lantern looked no bigger than a night-light. It swung from Mog's waist like a slipped halo.

"That's it," Alex said. "The crow's nest! She's done it."

"She's done half of it. She still has to come down," said Lenny.

"But that'll be easy, won't it?"

"*Dead* easy. She could do it in a couple of seconds."

Alex shuddered.

"I see what you mean. Hey—what's she doing now?"

"She seems to be buttoning up her shirt," I said.

"Eh?"

"That's what it looks like to me."

"And me," agreed Lenny.

"If I were up that high I'd leave it undone," Alex said. "Then if I fell the wind might catch in it like a parachute and slow me up."

"Fat chance."

"Well, it's possible. Isn't it, Genius?"

A gasp from the crowd cut off my reply.

"The lantern!" shrieked a girl. "She's dropped it!"

It fell like a star but much less smoothly—bouncing off hemp and wire till it ricocheted ablaze from the ship's bulwarks down to the concrete below. The sound and the trail of sparks faded. No one moved. Only Alex managed to whisper what terrified us all.

"Did . . . did Mog fall too?"

"Yippeeeeeeee . . .!"

Mog's cry made every kid jump. Like a trapeze artist in a power-cut circus she swept down from the crow's nest hand over hand. We couldn't see her but we could hear the hiss of her coming.

"Lights!" Howard bleated.

"Lights!" we all yelled.

They were switched on in time to illuminate Mog already back on deck with her arms stretched in a Big Top pose. The plastic bag had vanished.

"Mission accomplished, Mog," I murmured.

"What mission?" snarled Lenny. "She was just showing off. I've never seen anything so pointless in all my life. Suppose she'd slipped? It was a stupid thing to do. With your brains you ought to be able to see that. And don't tell me she was practising to be The Rectifier, either."

He turned away in disgust. On the far side of the water I could see Mr Skin. He was staring at Mog. Slowly, he shifted his gaze to the crow's nest then back again. Her climb didn't seem pointless to him.

Or to most of the kids round the pool. They clapped and cheered and whistled as if our school football team, captained by Mog, had just won the World Cup.

"Let's have an action replay, Mog!"

"One-handed this time!"

"With *no* hands this time!"

"The recorded highlights of Maritime Mog, steeple-jack of the seas!"

"Silence!"

It was an older, cigar-thickened version of Howard's voice that had spoken this time, a voice much more used to getting its way. Mr Bygrave had arrived. As he elbowed his way forward our uproar faded into a hush.

"Bet he's not keen on seeing his precious boy half-drowned," Alex laughed.

"He looks thrilled to bits with his precious boy," said Lenny. "What's up?" Mr Bygrave took no notice at all of the blankets draped round his son. From his crinkly, plastered-down hair to the last of his several chins, his face was one smug, ugly grin. To our astonishment, he put an arm round Howard's shoulders and pulled him up onto the plank over the swimming-pool.

"With a bit of luck this could be the other half of the drowning," Alex said. Howard seemed to be wondering the same thing.

"What's the matter, Dad?" he asked anxiously.

"The matter? Nothing's the matter. Everything's perfect, just perfect. I just want all your friends here to have a good look at you, lad."

"Why?"

Mr Bygrave's laugh was no more pleasant than his grin.

"Why, son? Because on Monday we're going on a little shopping trip, you and me. Just the two of us. And I'm going to buy you anything in the world you want. Do you hear? Anything at all. Whatever you choose, it's yours."

"Anything, Dad? Like my own racing car or a sailing dinghy?"

"My boy, certainly. Just name your present. Money no object. You deserve it."

"I do?"

"Of course you do. Don't you know why?"

"No. Unless . . . you don't mean . . ."

"I do, son. That's exactly what I mean."

From his top pocket, Mr Bygrave pulled out an envelope. It was yellow, the colour of a telegram.

"It's about the exam!" squeaked Howard.

"It's about a scholarship exam," said .Mr Bygrave. "Do you hear that, everyone? A scholarship that's been won by my son!"

"Dad!" Howard squealed. "I did it!"

"You did, boy. I always said you could and you did! And down below in the disco there's special champagne ice-cream for everyone!"

"I did it! I did it! I did it!"

"I think he did it," said Alex.

Beside me, Lenny shuffled his feet.

"Bad luck, Brains," he said.

"Oh," said Alex. "I hadn't thought of that. Bad luck, Brains. See you at the Comprehensive, then."

"Where Mog and Alex and me'll be going," Lenny added quickly.

"Funny really," Alex said. "I mean, I wouldn't have expected Howard to have done better than—"

"Shut up!" snapped Lenny.

"What? Oh . . . yes."

Lenny needn't have worried. Whatever anyone said I couldn't have felt worse. My chin trembled and there was a prickling behind my eyes. So it had all been wasted—hour after hour of study up in my room when I'd forced myself to ignore the noise of kids playing in the surrounding streets. For me it had been reading not buzzball. It had been maths and general knowledge instead of knock-down-ginger. And where had it got me? The Comprehensive. Just like the kids who ya-hoo'd around the neighbourhood from morning till night. I felt . . . mortified. That was the word for it. But what did knowing the word for it matter now? What did anything matter? I had a sudden vision of the sports photographs I'd passed when I followed the usher along that plush school corridor. Reflected in the glass of each one were my mum and dad with a disappointed look on their faces.

"Leave him," I heard Lenny say to Alex. "He'll need to get over it." That was why they disappeared below. Or maybe they were afraid of missing the special ice-cream.

I stared at the water, which was as flat and black as a piano top again, and at the streamers and plastic cups and funny hats that littered the deck all round it. Secretly, I'd never given up hope that the party wasn't for Howard or for Mog. I'd been hoping the celebrations were for me. For Brains. For Genius. For the scholarship boy who lived in a two-up and two-down terraced house on the wrong side of the heath with a postman for a dad and a mum who scrubbed floors when we were short of money. I threw back my head and howled from misery.

Howard was the scholarship boy not me. Howard, who'd only got Beta in the preliminary test.

And Mog was to blame.

What did it matter to me that the package really was evidence of tax-swindling? Why should I care that her mum was The Famous Rectifier? Would that get me any closer to becoming a professor or a brain surgeon or Prime Minister?

"Will you help me finish off the game we've been playing?" Mog had asked. Yes, Mog. I'd help all right. Hadn't I been helping you all along? Now it was time to help myself.

An Exit

Down the steps of the stern deckhouse was the captain's
dining-room and cabin. I knew this was where they'd be.
What I'd forgotten was that Mr Skin would be there too.
He was outside in the corridor like a sentry.

"What do you want?"

"I—I want to talk to Mr Bygrave."

"Very sorry. He's busy."

"He can't be—not for this. I've got something he'll
want to see."

"Like what?"

"It's for him. I'll only show him."

"Goodbye."

"But he *must* see what I've brought. He'll be grateful.
Really grateful." Mr Skin stared at me as if I were a dull
blot on a duller landscape. The jerk of his head was so
slight it was hard to tell if he'd moved at all but I felt it
from the scruff of my neck to the seat of my pants.

"Please," I begged. "It's important. He could go to
prison. I mean it. Here."

Fumbling, I jerked out the package. I unwrapped the
books and held them up.

"Now can I talk to Mr Bygrave?"

"Just where did you get those?" he hissed.

"I'll tell Mr Bygrave."

"You'll tell me."

"Mr Bygrave," I insisted.

His eyes were hard now and careful as if he weren't
sure of me. Was he wondering if I'd climbed up to the
crow's nest to fetch the parcel?

"Give them to me."

"No. They're for Mr Bygrave."

"I said give them to me . . . please."

"No."

So fast that a blink would have missed it, Mr Skin's hand shot out. I was jerked forward and lifted till the toecaps of my furry, Ben Gunn boots barely scraped the deck.

"*Do* drop the books," he said.

With a groan I let go. The account-books clattered at our feet.

"Thank you so much.'

He released me and stooped to pick them up. As he straightened the cabin-door opened. At once I clawed the books back from him.

"I've got to talk to you," I babbled. "About these. Don't you recognise them? They're your secret records. Every penny you've ever swindled from the taxman. Every loophole, every cheat—it's all here! And it's all in your handwriting . . . this is your handwriting, isn't it? I've brought them back to you! Both of them!"

"You don't say," said Mr Bygrave. "I think . . . I think you'd better come in."

The cabin was smaller than I expected, no bigger than my bedroom at home.

"Nice, isn't it?" said Howard.

He was sprawled in the captain's chair at the head of a long table.

"We've just been discussing my future, Dad and me," he explained.

He waved a hand airily at the oak panels all round us as though his future would be just as glossy. Instead of his Neptune outfit he now wore elegant slacks and a poshed-up fisherman's sweater worth a week's pay to a real fisherman.

"Sit down."

"Yes, sit down," said Mr Bygrave. "And hand me those books."

Howard's eyes widened.

"Hey, Dad! Are those the account-books—"

"Keep your mouth shut, Howard. This is between me and your pal here. He's going to tell me where he got them."

Mr Bygrave's voice was calm but his toby-jug face had that volcanic look Lenny had noticed.

"Well?"

"You—you've got them back now. That's enough isn't it? I've saved you hundreds of thousands of pounds by bringing them to you. Maybe more. That's worth something isn't it?"

"Like what?"

I blinked and bit my lip.

"Like the cost of a full six year scholarship. To the same school as Howard."

"For you?"

"For me," I said fiercely. "As a reward."

So quiet was the cabin you could have heard the tick of a wristwatch without lifting it to your ear. Mr Bygrave chewed at his cigar.

"A reward for property I've already got back? And which you shouldn't have had in the first place? You must think I'm soft, young squire. Unless, of course, you've taken the precaution of photocopying these accounts. No? I didn't think you would have. So you don't have much to bargain with, do you? Except, maybe, one thing. You could tell me who got hold of them. Because it wasn't you, that I'm sure of. But I'd very much like to meet the person who did get hold of them."

"I found them. I just . . . happened to find them."

"Certainly you did. You woke up one morning and there they were under your pillow. Brought personally by the sugar-plum fairy. These accounts, lad, were in a place as safe as the Bank of England and a lot more private. I put them there myself. Where no one could have stolen them . . . or nearly no one. The one person who might have been able to do it is dead."

"The Rectifier," Howard said.

"Or at any rate we've been led to believe he's dead. Perhaps we're all wrong. Perhaps that's only what we're supposed to believe. And now we've got you to help us find out the truth. How lucky we are . . . so who gave you the books?"

"No one. I don't remember."

"Skin," said Mr Bygrave. "Help him to remember. Help him gently at first but if he needs it help him harder."

"Please. Leave me alone. Please."

"Is your memory coming back?"

"I . . . I think so."

"Well then?"

"Mog," I said.

"What?"

"Mog. It was Mog. She gave them to me."

"Who?"

"Mog," said Howard. "Katharine Catley. You know, Dad—the girl you met in the museum. She's here at the party. I had to invite her because otherwise no one would . . . I mean, she's dead keen on The Rectifier. Practically president of his fan club."

"Yes. I recall that. The girl who's already in training for the day when she takes over from him—a kid who can fool a security man into thinking she's stolen a quarter of a million pound painting . . ."

Mr Bygrave thought about it.

"No," he said. "It's not possible. She's good but she's not that good. No kid could have taken these books from where I put them. She'd have to be The Rectifier already to do that. But maybe . . . maybe she's got some connection with The Rectifier . . ." He saw me flinch and knew he was right.

"So what's the connection? Do you need Skin's help to remember?"

"I . . . I'm not . . . not . . ."

"Skin, help him."

"Her mum," I said. "Mog's mum is The Rectifier."

"Her mum?"

"Hey, Dad! That is possible! There is something mysterious about Mog's mum. All the kids talk about it. She never seems to go out except late at night. And Mog's always talking about her as if she were some kind of Olympic athlete or . . ."

"Or The Rectifier," said Mr Bygrave.

Again he thought it over.

"No. There's something not quite right. Oh, I can see our guest here believes it—he's too scared stiff to tell lies. But somehow it doesn't fit. Not to my mind. Still, we'd better have a little talk with this Mog of yours."

"Let me fetch her, Dad. If you send Skin she'll be suspicious."

"Good thinking. Stay where you are, Skin."

"And you stay where you are," Howard said to me.

"I'm not going anywhere," I whispered.

Where could I go? Home, to tell Mum and Dad about the exam result? To the disco, to let Lenny and Alex know I'd betrayed our gang leader? There was nowhere for me to go now.

Not a word was said while we waited for Mog. With eyes like slits in a money-box Mr Bygrave leafed through the pages of the account-books. Mr Skin was as still as Dracula waiting for midnight. My brain became a television screen again but this time in sharp focus. The same film clip repeated itself endlessly: how the body of The Rectifier was found at last.

"In here?"

At Mog's voice all three of us looked up.

"Hello," she said. "You here as well, Genius? Hello, Mr Bygrave. Howard says you want to talk to me. What about?"

Howard sniggered.

"About your mum."

"My mum?"

"Amongst other things," said Mr Bygrave. "Leave this to me, Howard."

"But Dad—"

"Leave it to me, I said. Will your mum be collecting you tonight, young miss?"

"No. I'm going home with Lenny. Mum's at work."

"At this time of night?"

"She always works at this time of night."

"Really? What's her job, then? A burglar, perhaps?" Mog laughed.

"I often let people think it's something like that. They get so sniffy, you see, when they see her lying about the house most of the day. That's when she's tired out. She doesn't get home till it's nearly daylight—unless she's got an afternoon show as well, that is. She's a dancer."

"A dancer?" I said.

"That's right, Genius. I don't talk about it much because it seems so . . . well, *girlish*. She works in a night-club up in London. Modern dance, ballet, gymnastics: my mum can do it all though she says she's getting too old for dancing now. Sometimes when she gets home she's completely whacked-out. She's trying to save enough money to train for something else."

"You've never told me that."

"You've never asked. Neither have Lenny or Alex, I don't think. Whenever I mentioned my mum you all got awkward and embarrassed. But what's this got to do with you, Mr Bygrave?"

"Nothing at all. Unless your mum danced away from my house with these. They're private records of mine. Have you seen them before?"

Howard's dad jabbed a fat finger at the account-books which lay open on the table in front of him. Mog glanced at them and frowned.

"Private records? Should I have seen them before?"

"Your friend here says you gave them to him."

"Me? I did give him some books. In a plastic bag. They were part of a—of a game we've been playing. But they were old kids' stories of mine. Not these ones."

"Then one of you must be lying."

Mr Bygrave's eyes flicked from Mog to me. I knew exactly what he was asking himself: which of us needed the help of Mr Skin?

"You know you gave them to me, Mog," I said. "After we tried to hide the parcel down the Quaggy. I've had them ever since."

"Not these books, Genius. How could I have got hold of these? The ones we hid down the Quaggy were just story books. Don't you remember what happened? We . . . wait a minute, though. Let me think."

"Take your time," said Mr Bygrave.

I began to think too. It was as if my mind were linked to Mog's.

I remembered the dark, mouldering tunnel and Mog scrambling at the brickwork to make a hiding:place for the package. Then, in a hurry to get the package back, scrambling again . . . in not quite the same place. For a package that seemed to be much more tightly hidden.

A different package.

Also I remembered our rush out into the rain and our wait in the doorway for the motorbike to appear. Thirty seconds at least we'd held our breath. Long enough for our pursuer to discover the swop we'd made by mistake—a pursuer who was the one person able to steal the secret records of Howard Bygrave Senior and stash them in the Quaggy. How baffled he must have been to get Mog's fairy tales in exchange.

Mog was staring at him as if all those fairy tales had come true.

"I know what happened," she said. "No wonder we were chased afterwards. Have you worked it out, Genius?"

I nodded. It had taken me a long time but finally I'd worked it out.

The Rectifier, alias Mr Skin, reached for the account-books.

"I'll collect these," he said," for the Government. You won't be seeing me again, Mr Bygrave. But the Inland Revenue will be seeing you."

At the door he paused and looked back at Mog. His nothing-special face smiled suddenly.

"And thank you, Mog, for your . . . er . . . help. I'm sorry I must lock you in too but I never take chances with a getaway. Goodbye."

After the door had closed we heard the click of a brass hook in a brass catch and his footsteps fading.

"Are—are you all right, Dad?" asked Howard. "Dad, stop that shaking. *Please*, Dad."

Mr Bygrave's cigar, bitten through in his rage, bounced from the tabletop on to the floor. He spat what was left of it across the room along with every curse, oath and swearword we were ever likely to hear. Only when he'd run out of breath did he stop.

"Never mind, Dad," Howard soothed him. "At least I got my scholarship."

"A *half*-scholarship," snarled Mr Bygrave. "Let's have the truth. I've still got to find the money for the other half, remember—if I've got any money left at all when those tax vultures have finished with me."

"Okay, a *half*-scholarship," Howard admitted. "It's still better than you expected me to get."

"A half-scholarship?" I said. "So who got the full scholarship?" From the quayside came the kick-start growl of a thousand cc motor bike.

"Hey, Dad! That's my machine he's taking!"

"Nineteen hundred and ninety-five pounds' worth of machine . . . plus extras," said Mr Bygrave. "Just a drop in the ocean compared with what these books will cost me."

From the portholes we watched as The Rectifier revved the engine to commotion-pitch. Astride the machine he looked as tall as some of the stories about him. He lifted a glove to his vizor as if saluting us then accelerated away. Soon his tail-light had vanished into the darkness.

"Goodbye, Mr Rectifier-Skin," Mog said.

With her nose still pressed against the glass, she was the first to see the arrival of the brand new mail van.

"It's your dad, Genius. Wow! He's in a hurry. He's even left his lights on and the motor running. Wait a minute, your mum's with him too. She's waving something—something pretty exciting by the look of it. I think . . . yes! Definitely! It's a telegram!"

As she swung round her shout of delight turned to puzzlement.

"Genius, why are you looking like that? You've got what you always wanted! You've won the scholarship after all. There's nothing to cry about now!"

LEADFOOT

NICHOLAS FISK

There was a sudden roaring noise with yells and a jangle of music: the American convertible hurtled past, blaring its twin horns, bellowing chrome exhausts, screeching fat whitewalled tyres.

A drink can arced upwards, spinning and flashing. One of the men had thrown it.

There was an ugly, tinny thump as it smacked into the front apron of the Alvis...

'Leadfoot is pacy, gripping and involving.'
The Times

Post·A·Book

A Royal Mail service in association with the Book Marketing Council & The Booksellers Association.
Post-A-Book is a Post Office trademark.